JUDGE DREDD
THE MEDUSA SEED

THE MEDUSA SEED

Dave Stone

First published in 1994 by
Virgin Books
an imprint of Virgin Publishing Ltd
332 Ladbroke Grove
London W10 5AH

Typeset by CentraCet Ltd, Cambridge
Printed and bound in Great Britain by
Cox & Wyman Ltd, Reading, Berks

ISBN 0 352 32895 9

To the Public

Before going down among you to pull out your decaying teeth, your running ears, your tongues full of sores,
  Before breaking your putrid bones,
  Before opening your cholera-infested belly and taking out for use as fertilizer your too-fatted liver, your ignoble spleen and your diabetic kidneys,
  Before tearing out your ugly sexual organ, incontinent and slimy,
  Before extinguishing your appetite for beauty, ecstasy, sugar, philosophy, mathematical and poetic metaphysical pepper and cucumbers,
  Before disinfecting you with vitriol, cleansing you and shellacking you with passion,
  Before all that,
  We shall take a big antiseptic bath,
  And we warn you,
  We are murderers.

Manifesto signed by Ribemont-Dessaignes and read by seven people at the Grand Palais des Champs Elysées, Paris, 5th February 1920

And in 2116, the third stone from
the sun went crazy.

INITIAL TRAUMA

Burning Out

Two hours before his execution the killer requested spiritual counsel – something he had steadfastly refused before, for all that over months of psychiatric and psychological examination he had demonstrated an acute and unwavering religious mania. His hideous crimes, he maintained, had been the will of God: he was merely the instrument through which his god had worked, and such mundane terms as innocence or guilt were irrelevant.

Now, it was as though the actuality of his approaching death had finally broken him, panicked him, had finally instilled in him an acceptance of guilt and a desire for some last desperate act of contrition. A final confession before the vicar of the Lord.

Father Patrick Paul O'Donnell hurried through the dim brick and paint-walled corridors, footfalls ringing from pale green gloss and steel, the slick and liquid-looking concrete floor. The muffled clang of distant cell doors, the ambient susurration of the sleeping, the occasional faint and hollow scream more like the keening of some trapped and wounded animal than anything human. Low-wattage bulbs burned inside their lag-bolted wire cages like a fever.

1

A blunt man, O'Donnell, built from blocky fat and flesh; brittle strands of grey hair on a wide slick skull, pale thick sacs of skin wadded under the eyes. A whisky bloom.

Death Row. Animal house cages racked along the wall. The old, soured smells of sweat and scrim and semen, waste and excrement and desperation and fear soured and intermixed into something tangible, some miasmic gestalt entity of the caged, a thing in its own right and independent of the individual human components who might come and go.

And cool and still and perfectly calm. Nothing, even the certainty of death, can be terrifying for sustained periods of time; the mind simply switches it off. The inmates of the death house stirred list-lessly in their darkened cells, awake and waiting for the removal of one of their number: the only punc-tuation of activity in their day-to-day lives.

O'Donnell nodded to a guard who stood beside a heavy, chipped, dark green door set into the wall opposite the cages. An inset observation grating glowed with dim electric light.

'In here,' one of the guards said. 'Give you some privacy. He won't give you no trouble.' He grinned insinuatingly. 'The queer likes it young and fresh.'

He pulled the bolts and opened the door.

A tight, white room for the medical treatment and strip-searching of prisoners; a grubby patina of finger-marks accumulated on the walls. A heavy wooden chair and a dilapidated examination couch, its worn and yellowing canvas stained with bodily fluids and scarred with catgut darns.

The killer sat primly on this in laundered prison overalls, hands clasped on his bony knees. Rigid

2

steel restraints shackled wrists and ankles, connected by a length of leather-wrapped chain.

He smiled his gentle, cadaverous smile.

'Father,' he said.

'My . . .' O'Donnell's voice fractured. He looked into the killer's bruised and ancient eyes and was unable to complete the ritual address. 'My . . .'

The killer nodded kindly. His face was like a living skull.

The priest found that he was shaking. He pulled a grubby handkerchief from his pocket, pressed it to his wide and blocky brow, dabbed at his lips. It was as though, suddenly, that contact with the killer had earthed his soul. There was suddenly nothing inside him; he was hollowed out inside. And the ice-cold wind howled through him.

'I . . .' He tried to speak again, and it was as though he was speaking through borrowed meat. He was moving his mouth and respiring and making noises, but there was nothing alive inside. 'I – I have come to hear your confession. Your. I will hear your . . .'

And all the while the killer regarded him thoughtfully with his kindly, kindly eyes.

'Oh no,' the killer said mildly. It was as though, gently and with patient, indulgent love, he was correcting one of the more basic errors of a singularly backward child. 'No you haven't.

'You believe that you are clean in spirit. This is not so. You believe that your paltry God and your piss-poor Christ have the power to redeem or damn me. This is not so.'

The voice of the killer was soft and tremulous. It was without force. It was a voice of utter truth.

3

'You believe you have some intimation of God's glory. This is not so. Only I here know the sweet, pure value of sacrifice. Only I know. I who am so far above you. I *know* God. And God speaks to me.

'You are not here to receive my confession.' The killer blinked, slow and owlish. 'I am here to receive yours.'

Some ten minutes after Father Patrick Paul O'Donnell entered the examination room, the guards outside became aware of a violent commotion within. Said disturbance seemed so extreme that they entered immediately, batons at the ready, without first checking through the observation grille.

A wildly outflung fist caught one guard in the mouth, splitting his lip, a signet ring on one blunt finger shattering a tooth.

The second guard automatically clubbed his fellow's assailant in the small of the back, without noticeable effect.

Father Patrick Paul O'Donnell slapped and clawed at the bruised and bleeding face of the killer and then, snarling, gripped him by the throat, shook him like a terrier shakes a rat.

'How do you know?' he screamed in the killer's face. 'How did you *know?*'

And all the while the killer regarded him with a calm and smiling beatitude.

The killer was executed at one minute past midnight. The wounds inflicted on him by the priest – who by now was under light sedation and resting fitfully – were hastily cleaned and he was escorted to the

4

death chamber, limping slightly, though not from this or any recent injury.

After his arrest, examining surgeons had been surprised to find twenty-nine nails, needles and other items of a similar nature embedded in the subcutaneous flesh of his groin and genitals. A number of these were removed and found to be in various stages of oxidization: they had been inserted over the space of years if not decades.

Psychiatrists had theorised that this self-mutilation was simply part and parcel of the killer's sexual sadomasochism. Others held the reverse: that it was an attempt to mortify this, to purge himself of his perverted desires: a symbolic castration.

But the killer knew better.

In the same way that he had preyed upon children rather than adults, it was not that he had consciously *chosen* to do this – nor simply that the weak were easier prey – it was that there was no other choice. It was necessary. His God had commanded the blood sacrifice of innocents, had dictated their precise disposal, and had likewise provided the exact details for the killer's own self-mutilation. These were the things that must be done, and to the letter, and these things he had done.

The fact that these things gave the killer pleasure merely proved the unbounded and merciful love of his God.

When certain of the needles had been removed by the doctors he had been frantic. He had thought, then, that the undoing of his years of patient work would drive him mad. It was only after some months of surreptitiously re-inserting a length of straightened bedspring here, a purloined paper-fastener there, that he had at last regained some measure of inner peace.

There was still a large degree of apprehension, however: the poisitioning had to be scrupulously exact, and he was unsure whether these makeshift replacements would do the job. This was compounded by the fact that he had been forced to sterilise them with nothing more than a lighted match; the flesh of his groin was now inflamed and suppurating, the needles slipping and repositioning themselves constantly in the semi-solid and gangrenous pus. The killer had the uneasy feeling that all his efforts had been in vain.

All he could do was hope and pray. All he could do was wait.

When one imagines an electric chair one envisions something monolithic: some vast and towering black iron icon.

The reality is less prepossessing: square and blocky wood and frayed leather straps for forearms, calves and neck.

The chamber was brightly lit. Set into one wall, the dark glass of an observation window, dark shapes moving behind: the great and the good who had come to watch and gloat.

The Warden was here in his second-best suit, clutching a slip of pasteboard with pompous self-importance. His face glistened with an imbecilic and vaguely childish excitement: he was so proud.

The guards took the shackles from the killer's wrists, watchful in case of some last-minute and futile attempt at escape. The killer sat calmly down and smiled at them, gentle and kind.

The guards buckled the straps and fixed the earthing wire to his left big toe. They strapped the electrode cap to his head.

The warden nodded at him. 'Do you have anything to say?'

The killer considered this for a moment, then shook his head. The guards jammed the leather guard into his mouth, so that in spasm he would not sever his own tongue and cause unnecessary mess.

The guards stood back. The Warden read his pasteboard warrant and may God have mercy on your soul.

And then they left.

And four minutes later fifty thousand volts exploded through the killer, crawled down the main muscle mass of his back and arced down his spine – hit the needles that had been arranged over years with such precision.

The electrical explosion shorted out the execution chamber and half the jail.

The discharge crawled over the killer and set his skin on fire, deflected shrieking off the needles – and suddenly found itself directed at a right angle to reality.

Clawed at the fabric of space-time.

Opened, for a crucial nanosecond, a gateway.

SLICE ONE

There is a Happy Land

Sector 8, Mega-City One

In the shadows of a side-door under a vapour lamp advertising ENDOPHEMOROL, a Sirian in a suit of cured, stitched, human placenta passed a small polymer packet of white powder to a Practibrantic acolyte in a wooden suit. Dredd's hand twitched instinctively towards his Lawgiver.

'*Easy, Dredd,*' Control said in his ear. '*Remember where you are.*'

'I know it,' Dredd said. He swung the Lawmaster into the side alley, squeal-skidded the bike to a halt.

'Drokk off out of it,' he told the Sirian – who looked up into the Judge's basilisk snarl, decided not to risk it and slithered off into the darkness.

Dredd turned his attention to the Practibrantic, who as a human fell within his jurisdiction. He plucked the packet from an unresisting hand, pinched it open with gauntleted fingers and gingerly tasted the contents. 'Tate & Lyle refined. You got some primo powder here. Let's see your documentation.'

The man seemed perfectly calm. He pulled back

9

the segmented, varnished larch of his sleeve to reveal the barcode indelibly stamped on his forearm.

'Second generation Venus,' he said.

Dredd pulled a scanner from his belt and ran it over the stamp. It checked out. Creep was an offworld-born transient, worked the outer planet traverses as a bio-failsafe, the human equivalent of a canary in a coal-mine: alerting control systems to unknown factors which might damage perishable cargoes by the simple expedient of dropping dead. Practibrantics – a Venusian cult who firmly believed in an afterlife filled with nectar, prana and extremely accommodating houris and were thus prepared to die at any moment – were ideal for this sort of work.

'Okay.' Dredd put the scanner away and flipped the packet of sucrose back to the Venusian with a scowl and a spray of loose crystals. 'I've got your number. I've tagged your file. You set one foot outside the Hinterland, your feet don't touch, understand?'

'Yeh.' The Venusian risked an impudent grin. 'Got to let me go. Burns y'hole, yeh?'

Dredd considered this for a moment, then shot out a hand and hauled the Venusian up and off his feet by the scruff of the neck. 'Less of the lip, you little drokker,' he snarled into his face, fingers sinking hard enough to bruise. 'You might just meet someone with less self-control. Creep could get his head blown off in this sector and what with the restrictions on us we'd *never* find who did it, you got me?'

'Yeh,' the Venusian croaked, Practibrantic fatalism deserting him for a moment. 'I think I got you, yeh.'

10

Dredd dropped the Venusian in a small heap and swung the Lawmaster back out onto the street, scanning the Hinterland crowd with an angry, tight and absolute control.

Sector Eight, the Hinterland sector around Mega-City One spaceport, operated under international InterDep Law: much that was illegal in the surrounding city was freely available here – and much of the bigotry endemic to Mega-City One absent.

The legacy of the Rad Wars which had fried ninety per cent of the American continent and the subsequent horrors of fall-out had bred in the mega-cities an absolute intolerance of deviation from the genetic norm. Those with birth defects were terminated or eradicated immediately *ex utero*, mutants were lynched on sight and the mere apperance of an offworld alien could precipitate a full-scale species-riot.

There were inconsistencies, of course, as in all mindless bigotry: genetically based deviations like the Fattie cults were considered perfectly acceptable and even desirable, while those with Psi-talents and who were more or less human in appearance were afforded the ultimate status of Judges. But in general, in twenty-second century Mega-City One, overt genetic abnormalities had become the focus for all the phobias and spite that in other places and other times had been directed towards racialism or queer-bashing.

InterDep Law had no truck with any of this, being merely a basic world-wide consensus of what constituted a crime – and most of the world was far less extreme than Mega-City One. The Hinterland sectors of the world were melting-pots, and Sector

11

Eight, that four-mile-wide raised platform around the spaceport, was the one place in the Mega-City where aliens and mutants and other deviations could live: twenty-five square kilometres of smoke-houses and *kimu* parlours and vitriol bars, street vendors selling anything from hardcore bootleg holo-vids to dead meat sawed from an actual dead pig, to a vacuum-packed and freshly laundered reconditioned soul. Even the more basic varieties of keesh were sold openly here.

Traffic between the Hinterlands and the city proper was tightly controlled – and only a Senior Judge could police the Hinterland itself. Only a Senior Judge had the maturity to control impulses bred for and trained for all his life, and which would have a younger and more impetuous Judge automatically blowing everything and everyone in sight to drokk.

And even then, said Senior Judge was constantly in contact with Justice Department Control to keep him in check.

'You went close to the line back there, Dredd,' Control said. *'Dangerously close.'*

'What, me?' Dredd said. 'I was just giving the creep some friendly advice. That's what community policing's all about.'

Chakra Puja, MC1

In Mega-City One, in the Chakra Puja Block of Sector Eight, Sela opened the door of the cold room and, for an instant, automatically reeled back with alarm. The chill air carried the stink of mouldering decay; the spoiled-meat reek of the tomb.

12

Then this brief instant of animation left her. The dazed lassitude of the hypnotised or the heavily doped descended upon her again. She blinked, slow and imbecilic and faintly puzzled.

The Unbelievers had not controlled their base gluttony: they had stocked their larders with meats and tripes and lactic products that even the unenlightened Judges of the Mega-City proscribed. On the glorious day of the Occupation, the Faithful had found these refrigerated stores crammed with hanging carcasses and severed, fat-marbled limbs, strings of intestine stuffed with extruded offal, infertile avian embryos, slices of muscle tissue and a large flayed donkey, its flesh incised with the whorls and sigils of some sacrificial ritual.

The more zealous of the Faithful had wanted to dispose of this obscene provender straight away – but the Master, on due consideration, had forbidden this. It might fall into the wrong hands, or indeed mouths. He had thus ordered that these items remain safely where they were. He trusted his extensively conditioned minions to remain untempted by the pleasures of the flesh.

That had been two months ago – and by this point temptation was not much of an option. Saliva spurted and the gorge rose in Sela's throat. She vomited gently, almost absent-mindedly, then simply forgot about it and wandered through the hanging, decomposing meats, brushing vaguely and ineffectually at the stain on her front, and pulled a hessian sack of loose herbs from a shelf.

There had been a great many Unbelievers. The kitchen here was one of many: stainless steel and industrial, resembling that of a hotel. Sela measured

13

the herbs into the insulated urn and added boiling water, working like an automaton, her eyes heavy-lidded and vague and nothing behind them.

She placed the items on the trolley and wheeled it through the Level 15 corridors, feeling a vague, warm gratitude that the Master, who arranged every-thing, had arranged things so that she could see her husband during the day.

The truly Faithful, of course, were those who had joined the Master of their own free will, during the days in which he held sway in Mega-City One before being driven out by the forces of kevlar-clad dark-ness – those who had joyfully submitted to the hypnotic and narcotic rituals that had cleared their minds and set them on the proper path. These true disciples of the Master currently numbered five hundred and fifty.

There had been fifteen thousand Unbelievers living in the upper levels of the Chakra Puja block when the Faithful began their war of occupation. Heavy odds indeed – but the Faithful had prevailed in the knowledge that their Faith would gird them like an armour, and that the Holy Light that ban-ished the corrupt and illuminated them all would drive them through the heathen like a scourge of flails. The fact of ready access to a large number of Hondai AK209's – which rapid-fired microgrenades at a rate of seven hundred rounds a minute, plus optional clip-on FMJ auto attachments for close-quarter work – had absolutely nothing to do with it.

Less than seven hundred Unbelievers had sur-vived, and here the Master had shown his unending mercy. This filth would be converted, shown the error of its ways, taught to renounce their obscene alien gods and returned to the path of the Light.

Of course, once each of these new converts had undergone the procedure they were summarily despatched lest they fall back into old habits – but at least they were ensured of an eternal afterlife sitting at the right hand of the Master.

Sela and her husband Raan had joined the ranks of the Faithful together. The order operated on the tried and tested custom of the ages, in which the women got on with the cooking and the cleaning and the having of babies while the men did the real work, and quite right too – and Sela had watched and rejoiced as Raan had risen through the hierarchy to the exalted post of Principality, an operant conditioner working in the conversion chambers and barely one stratum down from the Master himself!

Sela pushed the trolley through the white-tiled corridor, passing a Soldier of the Light who lounged against a wall with his Hondai sloping down. She bowed her head, averted her dull eyes, as a woman must do in the presence of a man.

Casually, the soldier reached out a hand and began to rub her speculatively. She stayed still and waited for it to stop.

'Nice,' the soldier said. 'Lots of strong and muscle for a woman. Betcha like it good and hard, yeah?'

Women in the order tended to be used communally, though it was permissible for the more powerful members to lay exclusive claim to one by way of strategically placed bruises, which Sela sported on her upper arms and neck. She stayed still and kept her head down.

'Have to ask your man if I can have a go,' the

soldier said thoughtfully, gently shoving her on her way with the suggestion that he could shove a lot harder if he wanted to.

Down the corridor and through a swing-sprung set of double doors.

Psi Division, MC1

In a communal dayroom of Justice Department Psi Division, Karyn sat staring into her cold synthi-caf. She had been like this for hours now, hunched forward, immobile, a styrofoam cup cradled in her hands.

Around her people came and went. Crator had stayed for half an hour, skimming through the day's hard copies like an automaton and without the use of her hands. Moloch had come in to blow his top about something to do with the duty rosters, leaving in a fit of pique when he failed to elicit a response. Dexter had wandered in vaguely with his coverall smeared with vomit before a couple of auxiliaries came and led him away to clean him up.

Karyn noticed all of this only peripherally, through the tiny shred of awareness she had retained to monitor external stimuli. The rest of her was withdrawn and disassociated and locked off inside.

Psi talents operate via a number of processes, but can be divided into two general categories. The first is a simple reallocation of the brain's entire processing power toward some unorthodox task. A psychometrist, for example, upon entering a room, might receive a vision of an event that happened there – simply because the brain has extrapolated the events implicit in the exact arrangement of the objects within: this chair could only be positioned thus because of what happened minutes, or months, or even years before.

These talents were analogous to autism *savant* – where a child might demonstrate an absolute artistic genius, but be unable to respond to his name because the huge areas of his brain commonly used for social interaction have been reallocated to painting. These talents required no deviation from the human norm, and limited techniques for achieving them were taught to every Judge.

The second category required true mutation; senses and manipulations of an entirely different order: telekinesis, pyrokinesis, precognition . . . genuinely supranormal functions, as different from the common primary and secondary human functions as sight is from smell.

Those endowed with these functions were the true Psi Judges. Their mutations tended to follow a similar overall pattern – one or two specific talents tending to predominate in any individual – and there were strong grounds to support the theory that Psis were a distinct genetic strain in and of themselves: the next evolutionary step.

And a bigger collection of personality aberrations and psychiatric disorders you could never hope to meet.

It was not that Psis were naturally unstable. It was that every single one of them had grown up in a world where mutation was reviled. They had lived with the insults and the assaults and the baby-memories of the horror they had felt inside their parents, when they had discovered exactly what they

17

had birthed and had given them up to the Justice Department with a shudder.

Every Psi had grown up knowing that had their mutation taken the form of being able to move things with, say, an extra pair of hands rather than with their minds, they would have been put to death at birth.

They had grown up in a world of bigotry – and their psychic talents had made them feel it on a level far more basic and fundamental than could ever be conveyed by words or blows.

And they were expected to embrace and enforce this system of hatred. They were expected to be Judges. No other choice. Every single psychic talent the Justice Department knew about was integrated into the system in one form or another – and those who failed to make the grade were never heard from again.

Never.

A mind cannot function under such pressure for long. Psi Judges spent their lives under constant therapy and evaluation, and the Psi Division of Mega-City One resembled nothing so much as a mental hospital in which some of the inmates were allowed to carry guns.

And sooner or later, at some point or other, everybody cracked bigtime. The lucky ones lived to have their personalities reconstructed and were returned to active duty.

There were no inactive Psi Judges. None at all.

Psi Judge Karyn sat staring into her cold synthi-caf. She had been like this for hours now, hunched forward, immobile, styrofoam cup cradled in her hands.

Karyn was afraid. She was desperately afraid.
She was afraid that she was going mad.

Brit-Cit

'Did you see that?' Plainclothes Judge Treasure Steel
said. She swung her torch beam across the wall:
nothing but a tangle of misspelled graffiti and the
shattered remains of a halogen lamp in its wire cage.

'What?' Detective Judge Armitage of the Brit-Cit
CID swung his own torch round. 'I don't see anything. What did you see?'

'A woman.' Treasure considered the image etched
mnemonically on her memory. 'Pale face and jet-
black hair, kohl around the eyes, purple and gold
robes.' She pantomimed an artificially arch pose,
one hand toying with an imaginary ring on the third
finger of her left hand. 'She was there for a moment
– and then she was gone.'

'You're positive?' Armitage said.

'I'm sure. I don't think she was Brit-Cit – not *this*
century, anyway. She looked like something out of a
painting. One of the Pre-Raphaelite guys, y'know?'

Armitage nodded thoughtfully. 'Psychometric
flash, maybe – or maybe someone's buggering about
with trans-mat technology. Remember to have the
Psi and Tek people check it out.'

As they continued up the stairwell Treasure was
secretly pleased. Eighteen months ago, when she
was still a trainee under assessment, the Detective
Judge would probably have told her she was seeing
things – but time had meshed the two Judges'
personalities into a single effective unit. They knew
that their respective strengths complemented each

19

other, there was an implicit trust between them, and Armitage's casual acceptance of Treasure's unsubstantiated word was evidence of this.

The tip that they were currently following up was in fact almost entirely Treasure's. She was twenty years old, moved in other social circles than her superior officer, and had thus caught a reference off the streets that would have passed Armitage by.

'There's a buzz about some hardcore outfit running Tight White,' she had told him as they came on shift at the New Old Bailey, and explained the term.

'Oh drokk . . .' Armitage said. 'Something like that, they have to have protection from the big guys. We launch a trace operation, they whack us out the moment they hear about it. Then they just shut the lot down and resurface it somewhere else. How do we deal with something like that?'

In the end it had taken two months of trawling on the edge of Brit-Cit night culture before they ran down a possible location – all the while logging time on an unrelated long-haul case, all the while knowing that their actual quarry was still out there and operating. It was like wading in raw sewage.

Armitage had activated a couple of heavy-duty IDs, unshakeable and highly illegal even for a Judge, cutting off any possible backtrack to the Justice Department.

And, eventually, in a roundabout way, it had been intimated that they might find the, um, *service* they were looking for in a semi-derelict block in the North 15 sector.

They bought a couple of guns on the black market.

Chakra Puja, MC1

The conversion chambers took up a level of the block previously used for saunas and steam rooms – yet another proof of the Unbelievers' decadence. They had the distinct advantage, however, that they were comparatively easy to clean.

In the tight white cubicle, Raan ministered to the Unbeliever strapped to a reclining chair once used by a pedicurist (who with her scissors and with two unexploded slugs in her had given a Soldier of the Light a toe-job he would never forget before being taken down with a slash stick). The Unbeliever's flesh hung off him in loose, scabbed folds; he had once obviously been enormously fat before the starvation diet of his post-Occupation imprisonment.

He was naked. Blood streamed from sores and incisions and from the ruins of his mouth. His eyes were wide and very, very calm.

During one of his mellower moments, Raan had explained the function of the drugs used in conversion therapy: that they hypersensitised the pain-receptors whilst simultaneously suppressing specific involuntary reflexes, like tears or spasms which would trigger the release of natural endorphins into the bloodstream. Thus the subject was able to respond lucidly and seem perfectly calm whilst in the throes of excruciating agony.

'Do you see this "God" of yours for the abomination it truly is?' Raan was murmuring softly in the Unbeliever's ear. 'Do you renounce It and all Its works?'

'I renounce *Kloi Kloi Seki* and all Its works,' the

Unbeliever said calmly, if a little indistinctly. Blood bubbled in his throat.

'I don't believe you,' Raan whispered, and pressed the whining dental drill to a remaining tooth.

After a while he left the drill hanging, still running, from the Unbeliever's mouth and turned to see Sela. He raised an eyebrow.

'You're late,' he said mildly.

'I'm late.' Sela averted her eyes from her Husband.

Raan regarded her kindly. 'The Master has taught us the value of strict excretory continence, firm moral rectitude and of punctuality,' he said. 'I shall have to administer correction this evening. What have you brought for me?'

Head hung with shame, Sela pushed the trolley further into the room, for all the world a penitent bearing gifts for her Husband.

'I have brought you,' she said humbly, 'a willow-fine and cinnamon infusion and a toasted sesame-seed bap.'

Psi Division, MC1

The squeal of the alarm cut through the self-imposed mental blocks and Karyn spasmed, the burst cup dropping from her fingers to spill a brown film of synthi-caf across the slick polymer-tile floor.

Karyn wrenched herself back into full awareness. Her mind was fractured and flaring, screaming and jabbering in her head, but she gripped it with an iron control and forced herself to her feet.

She ran from the dayroom, colliding with a couple of beefy orderlies in the corridor outside as they hurried towards a door farther down: Moloch's private room.

The LED above the door was flashing yellow.

Something detonated in Karyn's head and suddenly all she wanted to do was hook her hands into claws and fling herself upon the orderlies, to tear their throats out with her snapping teeth and eat their *eyes* and . . .

'What's happening?' she said urgently as the orderlies shoved past her, running to keep up with them.

'Who cares?' one of them grunted brusquely. 'Little drokker's just throwing another stomm-fit. Drokk off and let us do our job, yeah?'

Psi Judge Moloch was probably the hardest individual to get along with in Karyn's section – which, given the state of Psis in general, was saying quite a lot. Without constant medication he tended to oscillate erratically between suicidal depression and a vicious, manic rage. Like most Psis, he spent the time in which he came into contact with Norms doped up to the eyeballs on an individually tailored cocktail of suppressants and endorphins, but within Psi Division itself he refused all drugs – averring that he'd rather crawl up the walls on a regular basis than do the zombie walk.

An orderly jammed her keycard into the slot by the door and it slid back on emergency override.

With the exception of events of this sort, a Psi Judge's quarters were utterly private. Karyn had never seen Moloch's rooms from the inside – and as she followed the orderlies in, as a wave of nausea broke over her, as she shuddered and jerked and tried to work her mouth, she was only aware of strobing, discrete, static images like snapshots:

a scattered mulch of discarded holo-vid cartridges, data wafers and ancient paperbacks, their spines broken and their covers stained and ripped. Visible titles included: *Briefing for a Descent into Hell*, *A Cure for Cancer*, *The Eye of the Lens*, *The Iliad*, *Paradise Lost*, *Deathmasques* (this, obviously, barely opened and then hurled away with some force) and *Camp Concentration*;

a small collection of broadly humanoid figures ranging from proprietary children's toys to an antique, jointed, wooden, artist's marionette, twisted into postures suggesting agony, uncontrollable laughter, orgasm. In particular, a stuffed doll skinned with soft black polished leather. Scrawled across its slick and pendulous belly, in red lipstick, a single word: SUCK;

a monochrome poster of Greta Garbo, the screen actress, reclining upon something dark and diaphanous and yearning, upward, toward something out-of-shot. Mismatched four-colour facial features, ripped from other sources and pasted down made her face something crazed and grinning and vulpine;

Moloch on an unmade mattress, tangled in grubby, sweaty sheets and blankets: thin and pale and struggling with the orderlies as they pinned him down and gave him a hypo, haemorrhaging from nose and eyes and screaming the same word over and over and *over* again: 'Mouth! Mouth! Mouth! Mouth! Mouth!'

Primary disruptions

It started small and slow. In the foetid, mutagen-shrouded jungles of Madagascar, the air scintillated: swirls of variegated primary light enveloping a four-foot-wide arachnid in the process of laying its eggs in the hairless living flesh of a marmoset – both collapsing in an accelerated decay and in a matter of seconds to leave white bone and a chitinous husk.

Sector 8, MC1

Dredd gunned the Lawmaster past an overcrowded servo-powered rickshaw (a brood-family of slimy obloids following him with startled, segmented, insectoid eyes) and cruised through the Hinterland streets, flipping his attention more or less at random:

an elderly and ectomorphic Earthman in battered stovepipe hat and frock coat, turning the handle on a baroque barrel-organ dating back centuries, its workings replaced by solid-state synth circuitry. A cyber-modified monkey on a chain capered, LED eyes glowing redly. The original organic tissue was dead and partially mummified;

before a steam-shrouded *kimu* stand, a scaly humanoid in silver-sheen living body-armour waved his hands and argued with a pale, slick globe encased in meat and oxidizing iron;

in a boarded-up doorway, living clockwork automata played some indefinable offworld game with scattered, polished knuckle-bones, chittering amongst themselves in an alien language of ticks and rattles and clicks while a scarred and battered Titanian Jackboxer looked on watchfully, the vidcams in

25

his (he was obviously male) prosthetic head plugged directly into the brain tissue nestled in his abdomen in lieu of bowel organs, and –

It was like spotting English characters in a page of Hondo ideograms: it blazed out at you. An Earthman in a grubby Mega-City-cut overcoat, furtively winding through the pedway crowd. Overcoat wrapped around him, masking something clutched to his chest through the pockets. He had not yet registered the Judge, who was at this point some fifty metres up the street and partially hidden by the chaotic Hinterland traffic.

'I think I got a live one,' Dredd told Control. 'Run me a make.'

A brief flicker in his vision as Control accessed his cybernetic eyes and zoomed in on the target for a microsecond to scan and factor the visible facial features.

The man was heading for a high-rise, the Chakra Puja block, the upper levels of which were completely taken over by some offworld religious order: basic rockcrete obscured by a painted bas-relief fresco depicting the eating of some towering multi-armed alien creature by a mass of neotonic and razor-toothed larvae. The lower levels were taken up by storefronts, amongst them the polarised plate glass of a bar in which vapour signs flared: CAPONE'S. The man darted nervously into the bar.

'*Arlo Marcus Jenks,*' Control said in Dredd's ear. '*Mega-City citizen. Four years cube-time. Warrants outstanding: two counts armed robbery, four counts proscribed substance abuse, one count homicide. Dropped out of sight six months ago after he cut the barcode off a spacer. You can go for it.*'

26

'Gotcha.' Dredd hit the accelerator and swung across the street, sidewiping a canopied tricycle and pitching its corpulent rider into a cart of overripe Centauran *zumi* fruit with a de-velocipeded squeak. As the Lawmaster roared for the bar, shots sounded from within.

Primary disruptions

In the nuclear deserts south of Chicago, a pack of slightly scorched black-plague rats spontaneously generated from nowhere. Radiation and the unfiltered sun killed or sterilised the majority in a matter of hours, but two – a breeding pair, the female gravid with young, survived to reach the city.

Brit-Cit

A small pool of some hydrocarbon-based fluid had been spilled across the undressed rockcrete floor of the corridor and set alight; pale blue vapour-flame guttered.

There was nothing discernible to the untrained and casual observer, but their Judge-trained, fine-tuned instincts made them aware of the pin-point microcameras in the walls, a minute and subtle change in background ionisation. They were being scanned. They were being watched.

Armitage and Steel went into their act.

'This damn thing better be worth the candle,' Armitage slurred in half-cut, huntin'-shootin'-fishin' tones while affecting a limp and clumping club-footed on his cane. 'Damn gout's playing me up like the buggery.' His cover ID was that of a colonel

27

from the Turkmenistan Protectorates – the area around the former Central Asian city of Askhabad, occupied by Surrey New Raj military forces fleeing across Eurasia in sub-orbital transports from the British Civil War and the subsequent Consolidation, and who had founded a tenacious, if compact, colonial culture. The protectorates maintained strong links with Brit-Cit – although they regarded the huge city-state covering the entire south of England as now merely a far-flung outpost of a slightly relocated 'British' Empire, of which they themselves were the centre.

Armitage was splendid in full dress-uniform of royal blue silk, crawling with frogging and braid, a ceremonial sabre hanging from his blancoed belt. He had taken advantage of a couple of months of covert operations to cultivate a dashing set of mutton-chop whiskers. His ID had officially recognised and backdated diplomatic immunity, thus making purported criminal activity more plausible, and making heavy-duty checks upon said ID well-nigh impossible.

Treasure was currently purporting to be an escort from a high-class agency specialising in 'well-bred ladies for the accompaniment of a discerning clientele', a true escort agency and strictly legitimate in the sense that, say, an aromatherapic massage in a health spa is legitimate compared to a couple of girls up the back stairs with a towel.

The agency was in fact a 'phantom' operated by some slightly dubious people with whom Armitage had contacts – that is, it was a business concern which existed in every single sense and detail other than the physically actual, as the putative shareholders in said concern would ultimately find out. The operators of the scam – who, like most confidence artists, were sophisticated and fundamentally non-violent – had been horrified to learn of the activities that the two Judges were investigating, and had integrated the details of an extra employee into their set-up like a shot. The cover was as rock-solid and unshakeable as hardcore hacking and a strategically placed system of plants could make it.

Treasure stumbled against her superior officer as though slightly intoxicated, stroked his whiskers and giggled. The go-nomad delphic styles currently affected by the better-bred young ladies of Brit-Cit were slightly dishevelled. Every nuance and inflection radiated a self-centred and incredibly dumb sense of superiority. 'Don't worry. It'll be nice. It's going to be so *nice*.'

Treasure, Armitage thought, was overdoing it a bit.

A narrow and featureless if filthy door. They stood before it and it slid back silently.

A small, lobby-like cubicle, walled with polished brass and rose-shot marble, and utterly incongruous with the squalor of the corridor outside. Again they waited, knowing that the ID searches and security scans were being run. Both noticed that every surface of the cubicle was slick and extremely easy to clean. This was where they would suddenly find out if their covers were deep enough for long enough.

A section of wall slid back. The concierge stepped forward in his tight and pristine dinner dress.

'Welcome.' He regarded them with a split-second of sardonic contempt before adopting a patina of servility. 'It is always a pleasure to greet such honoured and patently solvent guests.'

29

Primary disruptions

And in the skies above Simba City a burning woman was seen for an instant: arms thrown theatrically akimbo like some expressionistic Winged Victory of Samathrace. Her eyes were sad and perfectly calm.

Chakra Puja, MC1

Sela looked down at the bruises, livid red and blue in the flesh above the swell of her breast. An observer would see that they formed an upside-down letter P. It was upside-down so that she could read it.

P for Punctuality. She tried to fix it in her head, repeating it over and over again subvocally, because she was very dim and she would probably just forget if she didn't.

'I hope and trust this reminder will suffice,' Raan had said gently as he pressed his thumb hard and precise into her again and again and again. 'I'll have to cut it into you if it doesn't.'

Someone was slapping at her face. She resurfaced from her self-hypnotic torpor.

'Take the child,' Rann was saying. 'I have work to perform.'

He thrust little Kelli into her arms. The child looked up at her with his bright, wide eyes – and for a moment she found herself holding the child to her with a vice-like, hysterical grip, the explosion of loss and love inside her making her want to scream, before the half-stifled child began to struggle.

She let the child go.

'What did you learn today?' she asked him.

The child regarded her with a contempt that, for an instant, pierced her heart before she remembered that this was precisely what she deserved. She had served her function when she had borne him and suckled him, and now at four years old he had naturally outgrown such childish and bestial attachments. She was ashamed to have embarrassed him by this unseemly show of feminine weakness.

'I learnt the three basic tenets of the True Faith,' the child explained vaguely, as though humouring an outgrown and irritating pet.

Sela nodded solemnly. This was the exact same answer the child had made for the six months –

Six months? *Oh Grud I thought I could but how could I let them they did this thing to him I let them do it and they did it again and again and again and*

– for the six months since the Master had brought the Light into their eyes and lives. Every day the children were taught the True Faith – and at the start of every day their minds were cleared so that they could learn it afresh, which was just as it should be. The constant repetition would burn it into their minds forever.

The child lapsed into a sullen silence. Sela turned her dull eyes to those around her.

The Faithful slept communally though divided more or less into family groups. The largest chapel of the Unbelievers had been set aside for this purpose and adapted to their needs.

It was almost time for the Nocturne Ceremonies. Raan, with the other Principalities, was picking his way through the candles and the sigils and the murmuring figures as they sprawled upon their bedrolls, making his way towards the dais and altar

31

at which the Master would duly appear – once he had sufficiently rested and invigorated himself with his Brides of the day.

Sela herself had been one of the Brides on two occasions, and she rejoiced at the memory of it, while somehow being unable to quite remember anything that had actually happened.

Sela was at peace. Save for the Soldiers of the Light who patrolled the deserted corridors of the block and who stood sentry against all possible incursion from the sector outside, all of the Faithful were here. Her family was here.

Save for the occasional squall of a baby too young to exercise a proper control, the Faithful were hushed, waiting for the Word.

Several of the Principalities now moved through the crowd, distributing chemically impregnated eucharist wafers from bags, placing them on tongues to dissolve. She awaited her turn, and the arrival of the Master.

And then the muffled gunfire.

And all Sheol broke loose.

Primary disruptions

And in the stratosphere over Lhasa, several fragmented lumps of metal appeared and continued under their own momentum before falling like shooting stars. Detailed analysis, had such been available in this instant and at this altitude, would have revealed them as the exploded remains of certain components of a USAF F-111 dating from the latter half of the twentieth century.

Vestigial remains of fissionable material from a

*covert nuclear warhead would, over the next year,
cause lung- and related cancers in more than fifteen
thousand individuals throughout the world – relocat-
ing a minuscule proportion of the deaths caused by
most of said material, when the F-111 was originally
shot down by friendly fire SAMs in 1971.*

Sector 8 (Chakra Puja), MC1

Justice Department Lawmasters are packed with
sensors and compensatory systems designed to mini-
malise unnecessary harm to innocent bystanders.
Dredd hit the plate-glass window and burst through
it with an explosion of polarised silicates, the Lawmaster factoring the heat-signatures of those inside
and venting a couple of retros to hit the floor of the
bar and powerslide, shrieking to a dead stop millimetres from a couple of patrons cowering under a
table.

The bar was built along the lines of a 1930s
speakeasy by an interior designer with no sense of
history, taste or interior design: alcoves in the wall
contained animatronic gangsters ratcheting their cir-
cular-magazined Thompson sub-machine guns
through Hollywood moves; a stage, where Carmen
Miranda banana-costumed dancers pressed themselves back against a wall, back-projected with a
swinging big band. A 30s-model Ford with running
boards hung precariously by wires.

Arlo Marcus Jenks was at the bar, jamming the
snout of a flenser into the face of a waistcoated
barman and screaming about how he, the barman,
should do it *now*. A man and a woman lay sprawled

by him, gaping, cauterised holes blown through them: shot so they would just get out of his way.

He had not reacted at all to Dredd's arrival. He was up on something and lost in his own private world.

'*Do* it!' he shrieked at the bartender. 'Do it *now!* I want you to do it and *do* it and . . .'

Dredd climbed off the Lawmaster and glanced down at the couple under the table: a youngish and sallow-faced exec and a paid escort who had dropped her bimbo-act. They looked up at him.

'Mind my bike, yeah?' he said.

Smoothly he strolled through the panicked clientele to the bar, grabbed Arlo Marcus Jenks by his tangled hair and slammed his face into the bartop. A crack, a wet snap and a small spray of blood.

Arlo Marcus Jenks slumped unconscious. The shaken barman pulled a towel from the rail and pressed it to his sweaty face. 'I *tried* to tell him we don't have cash in them.' He indicated an antique brass cash-register. 'We only take credit chips. I tried to tell him. He wouldn't . . .'

Dredd became aware of a presence behind him and turned to face a portly, blustering man in a stripy suit and white fedora and spats – obviously intended to convey gangsterism, but in fact merely conveying dressing up ineptly and feeling a bit of a fool. He seemed angry.

'What do *you* want?' Dredd said.

'Mico Ricci. I own this place.' Mico Ricci who owned this place waved a hand at the idling Lawmaster and the shattered window, the vapour sign still hanging in the air, warped and flaring and now reading: SYSTEM ERROR 3.1.

34

'That was genuine silicon,' he said belligerently. 'Two thousand creds' worth of genuine silicon. I want compensation.'

'Don't push your luck.' Dredd scanned the bar interior. 'You're selling ethanol. In Mega-City One that's *verboten*. How would you like it if I stationed a couple of Judges outside full-time to check for Mega-City cits coming in and out? We'd have to check everybody. We might have to take genetic samples, just to be sure.'

'I think our Justice Department does a wonderful job,' Mico Ricci who owned this place said promptly.

Dredd headed for the door, dragging the unconscious Jenks. The Lawmaster powered up and headed for the hole in the window on AI automatic.

Outside a small crowd of onlookers was dispersing. Dredd dragged Jenks to a Justice Department holding post and cuffed him to await an h-wagon.

He switched in his throat mike. 'Problem sorted, Control. Add another count of attempted armed robbery. Fifteen years. I'm outside Chakra Puja Block and am continuing on . . .'

It was entirely instinctive: an instant, automatic reaction to some stimulus on the extreme edge of line-of-sight, triggering an automatic response in the same way that a sparrow might respond to the shadow of a hawk. An instant awareness of a dark shape in the window half-way up the block – and then he was diving for cover as the explosive slugs stitched across the pedway.

Primary disruptions

And across the world, and largely unnoticed, discrete physical objects from the molecular level up appear and disappear and transmute. Ghost voices and images sleet through the real like static on a badly tuned TV. Ripples in the fabric of space-time.

Something coming.

Sector 8, (Chakra Puja), MC1

Later, when Justice Department Teks sliced and decoded their dead minds, it was discovered that the Soldiers of the Light had undergone extensive conditioning, their nervous systems streamlined, programmed to respond instantly and automatically to external stimuli falling within a limited set of parameters.

A Justice Department Lawmaster attacking Chakra Puja Block, even those ground-floor sections unoccupied by the Faithful, fell within those parameters.

Arlo Marcus Jenks went down in pieces, spattering Dredd with intestine and a section of stomach as he dived for the cover of an open garbage skip, vaulting the rim and crunching into a rotting mulch of packaging, half-eaten food and excrement. Some liquid substance – either a potable for or the waste matter of some alien lifeform inimical to human beings – ate through the polymer over his left thigh with a hiss.

Around him, explosive slugs tore through the crowd as they shrieked and stampeded.

36

Dredd craned his neck and scanned the block. Dark figures blazed away from maybe fifteen open windows. He steadied his Lawgiver on the sill of the skip and loosed a couple of shots: a figure jerked back to be lost from sight with a distant shriek and a spraying tracer-arc of slugs.

The Lawmaster arrived, squealed to a stop before the skip.

'Bike!' Dredd roared. 'Fifteen targets! High elevation! Hi-ex!'

'Complying.' The bike tracked its integral cannon upwards.

Primary distruptions

And in the Hives of Hondo City, an exec lurches back with a cry from a geisha as she crumbles in accelerated decay. In Europa, four hundred citizens spontaneously blister and retch psychosomatically, their symptoms remarkably similar to those produced by chlorine-based mustard gas, of which there is no subsequent trace. In New Jerusalem the icons are running with blood.

The Trenches, MC1

In the post-Rad War chaos, when the survivors had consolidated themselves into the vast population centres of the mega-city states, the wrecked and irradiated vestiges of Old New York had posed a slight problem: too extensive to demolish, too intricately degenerate to cleanse, they proved to be uninhabitable in the terms of the new and radically simplified Judge-based world order.

The solution, in the end, had been simple. Over the space of bare months, utilising prototype transmute-technology and drawing on the raw material resources of half a continent, they had simply rockcreted over vast areas of the city. Those original inhabitants who were genetically clean were evacuated, those who were not, and who tried to escape as the huge construction rigs advanced and covered the sky, were wiped out by hunter-killer squads of Judges – and those who remained were left to die, or to eke out whatever remained of their lives in the perpetual and infection-ridden darkness.

These roofs, as Mega-City One took form on top of them, effectively became the new ground level: City Bottom. And as the city grew up and ever upwards, this ground level had become choked with the detritus of the city above.

A sludge of perishable garbage decomposed over years; the protruding, skeletal tangle of the unrotted. The lower levels of the blocks themselves were no-go areas, sealed off from the levels above. The majority of the interways and access ramps this far down were derelict, those still serviceable only used by the Judges who policed these levels – not through any sense of enforcing some democratic law for all, but merely to prevent the spread of their inhabitants and their Byzantine intergang wars spreading upwards.

The average age of death here was fourteen – the bare minimum level by which human beings as a group can breed to any extent before they die, and thus produce a relatively stable system. The lost children crawled through the dark and killed and ate each other and bred.

These areas of City Bottom were called the Trenches.

Ani cut a hole and pulled the lights out, bolting them. They needed no cooking and they would rot first.

Then he sliced into the muscle, working quickly and cleanly, stuffing the bloody lumps into his saltsack.

The scavengers had the scent.

He saw them as he made the incision in the laterally incised, flayed thigh to pull out the main mass of the bone. Torchlight, winding through the tangle of burnt-out fliers dumped decades before.

They came through the wreckage: four of them, three boys and a girl trailing behind, two of the boys shielding her from any danger. A breeding group. A tribe. The scratches made in their faces and kept permanently open, encrusted and weeping – spiral whorls on foreheads and over cheekbones.

Ani knew their rituals.

Their leader, the largest, stood ready. Ani saw the muscle bulging in his good arm. With his atrophied arm, he held out a torch.

It is possible that certain rituals are basic to human beings, ingrained in the back-brain and resurfacing when some imposed overall system of behaviour is absent. Alternatively, and far more plausibly, it is simply a matter of chance: this has been done, and at some other point, over the tens of thousands of years that human beings have been alive and inter-acting, this has been done before.

Either way, this particular tribe had evolved rituals remarkably similar to the plains-dwelling Indians of centuries before. A means of showing strength on a higher level than simple aggression.

The leader of the tribe held out his torch, and Ani knew that this was their hunting ground, and he knew their rituals. He had saved the intestines of his kill.

Slowly he pulled them through the flame of the torch, cooking the semi-digested matter inside. Then he squatted and placed them between himself and the leader.

The leader squatted, facing him. The two boys stood back, guarding the girl – though Ani knew that if he lost this contest they would instantly fall upon him.

Together, Ani and the leader of the tribe took an end of intestine in each of their mouths, and swallowed. And swallowed. And swallowed. Taking the string into themselves until their faces were only a matter of inches apart.

This was the dangerous part. Had the leader been less honourable, he would have bitten down and achieved some purchase . . . but he did not.

Ani, who was not of their tribe, had no such compunction. He bit down and pulled, swallowing and swallowing and swallowing until he had pulled the entire length from the leader's stomach and taken it into himself.

The leader glared at him. For an endless moment Ani thought he was going to attack – but, at last, his sense of honour won out. He nodded.

Ani completed his butchery of the boy he had killed, conspicuously leaving choice cuts on the carcass. Then he backed off.

He kept his eye on the scavenger tribe until they

fell upon the remains of his kill, then headed off through the maze of the Trench, heading for his lair.

Primary disruptions (MC1)

And in Sector 37, Psi Judge Trask sits in the kitchen of a conapt (where he has been establishing exactly why a young mother did for her spouse, her two infant children and then herself with a packet of drain cleaner) – the leggings of his uniform around his ankles, smearing a portion of munce he has found in the refrigerator around his mouth and crooning, 'So nice, so nice . . .' over and over again.

Brit-Cit

A chamber crawling with baroque gilt enclosing huge plate mirrors on the walls. Chandeliers twinkled, hanging from the vaulted roof.

Diners sat at tables, tucking in: richly clad and wealthy and elegant. Conversation was mannered and subdued. Waiters shuttled from the kitchens to the tables like schooners under full sail – and it would take a second glance to register that some of them simply wandered the room watchfully, hands hovering over their breast pockets.

The place stank of a sweaty, guilty, almost sexual excitement, as though this patina of elegance was merely the crust over some pulsing and feverish infection.

'Table for two,' Armitage said.

The concierge nodded and led them to a table for two. Armitage examined the cutlery minutely, then finally put it down again grudgingly with a grunt as though awarding its scalpel-clean shine a barely passing mark.

A waiter appeared. 'Sir. Madam. May I take your order?'

'I want Tight White,' Treasure said with a slightly nervous bravado, like a child ordering a beer for the first time.

The waiter nodded. 'Yes. I gather that the term has some popularity with the younger generation. Our, ah, *suppliers* if you will. We, however, prefer the more traditional term of long veal.'

'Damn right,' Armitage grunted. 'That's what we called it in my day, and I see no reason to change it now. Long veal with all the trimmings.'

'Something to drink while your order is prepared?' said the waiter.

Armitage sipped a port and brandy while Treasure finessed her way through a bottle of vintage champagne she had drunkenly insisted on ordering, barely touching a drop and giggling about how the bubbles tickled her nose. All the while they scanned the chamber, taking in the clientele and the security guards and tagging the danger-men, communicating with each other by the barest flicker of their eyes.

Fifteen minutes later their waiter swung his way through the tables, a platter with a silver-plated dome held over his head. He placed it upon the table, swept the dome up with a small flourish. 'Sir, Madam. Your long veal.'

It was surrounded by glazed carrots, roast potatoes and mange tout. Its skin was charred to a golden and truffle-pocked crackling. There was an apple in its little mouth.

Armitage looked at it for a moment, sniffed at it suspiciously and blew his top.

'This long veal is *off!*' he roared. Across the chamber, tasteful conversation broke off and heads turned to regard this furious bewhiskered man of military bearing with alarm.

'Sir?' The waiter seemed suddenly nervous. 'I'm afraid I don't quite – '

'You understand me perfectly well, laddie,' Armitage thundered, controlling his breathing, so that his face reddened apoplectically. 'You think that because I'm from the Protectorates you can palm me off with any old leftovers you might happen to have lying around.' He glowered up at the nonplussed waiter and made a vein throb on his head. 'I've been eating long veal since before you were a twinkle in your father's kneecaps, laddie,' he said murderously, prodding the thing upon the platter, 'and I have no idea when *this* died – but it certainly wasn't alive yesterday.'

The waiter bristled, almost lost his composure before visibly restraining himself. 'I can assure you, sir, that . . .'

'You'll assure me nothing, laddie.' Armitage swept the platter off the table and lumbered to his feet, grabbing an obviously bewildered and embarrassed Treasure by the arm. 'Come, child, we'll eat elsewhere. There are other places.'

'I'm afraid,' the waiter said with extreme control, 'that we have the, ah, *monopoly* on this particular . . .'

During the course of this most distressing scene, the concierge had been conferring with an ectomorphic and middle-aged man in splendid full dinner

43

dress. This latter man left his table and took the
waiter lightly by the arm. 'It's perfectly all right,
Globes. I'll deal with this.'

He turned to regard Armitage with calm courtesy,
the perfect host. 'I gather there is a problem, sir?'

'Damn right,' Armitage growled. 'I take it that
you are the owner of this establishment?'

The newcomer nodded. 'I am.'

'That's all I wanted to know.'

The guns the Judges had obtained on the black
market were of the sort used almost exclusively by
terrorists: entirely chemical and mechanical in operation, built entirely from polymers and ceramics,
utterly undetectable by conventional security systems. Armitage hauled out his gun and shot a couple
of waiters who were going for theirs.

Treasure was dealing with a couple more, heading
for the door in a running crouch to block it off and
prevent escape by the panicked clientele.

Armitage, meanwhile, broke a couple of teeth
pistol-whipping the still-hovering waiter out of the
way, pulled his ceremonial sabre from its scabbard
with his free hand and laid the flat of it across the
restaurant owner's twitching neck.

'Do not pass go,' he said. 'Do not collect two
hundred creds.'

Primary disruptions (MC1)

*And in the Mega-City One Psi Division, as the
alarms shriek around them, orderlies stabilise the
haemorrhaging Psi Judge Moloch, finally turn to
see the shaking, jerking, clawing Karyn and ad-*

minister anti-shock drugs and Psi-suppressants and pheno-barbitone.

And one by one, throughout Psi Division, other alarms add themselves to the clamour.

Sector 8 (Chakra Puja), MC1

The Lawmaster opened up and cut a swathe across the block, a string of detonations hurling burning bodies from the windows to fall to the street.

Dredd swung himself from the skip, scanning the burning holes in the block for movement. The street was now deserted except for maybe fifty feebly flopping wounded and the dead. There was a distant sound of shouting and crashing as those fleeing disrupted the surrounding streets.

The block loomed silent. The Lawmaster by him ratcheted its guns back and forth, automatically scanning for potential threats.

Dredd cut in his mike. 'Control? You getting all this?'

'*We got it,*' the voice of Control said. '*It's your call, Dredd. What do you want?*'

'I want this area locked off. Grud only knows how many of the drokkers are up there. I want Shok-Tac and Anti-Terrorist and drokk the InterDep restrictions.'

'*You got it, Dredd. We're hitting the go-switch now. ETA in five to ten.*'

'Good enough.' Dredd noted the bas-relief designs that crawled over Chakra Puja Block with distaste. 'Seems to be some sort of religion involved here, probably offworld. Check the databases and get me a line on these creeps.'

Dredd climbed onto the Lawmaster and gunned it to life, swung across the street to a slightly less exposed position – and the demolition charges strung through the entire lower level of Chakra Puja Block detonated.

The force of the blast flipped the Lawmaster onto its back and it skidded, shattering Dredd's right leg with a wet and ragged crunch.

Primary disruptions

Reality fragmentation. Fractures in space/time. Holes are opening and sicking things out. Everything lost and dislocated and adrift in time sicked back into this continuum with a bang.

Reality-quake coming. It's all coming back.

The Trenches, MC1

Ani clambered over the twisted iron mass of scaffolding, swung himself up onto the derelict remains of a pedway. Along this, it was an almost clear run to his lair: a large, hollow polymer cast of the head of an inanely grinning frog, the remains of some long-discarded animatronic advertising hoarding, wedged between a ruptured and ketone-reeking tanker trailer and the vertical edge of a block.

Cautiously, senses alert for movement in the surrounding darkness, Ani scrambled across the crumbling rockcrete.

The explosion set him on fire and knocked him off the pedway, to fall thirty feet and hit a loose slope of mulch and artificial shale, breaking his spine. Free hydrocarbons produced by decomposing garbage burst into flame.

The pain was immense – and then it simply shut down. It had passed beyond the point where the boy's overloaded neurosystem could recognise it as such.

Ani lay sprawled and burning on his back, paralysed from the waist down. Automatically he breathed in flame, instantly vaporised saliva and mucus exploding his lungs. In the saltbags hung from him, freshly butchered meat roasted with his own.

And above him, on the pedway, the figure who had exploded out of nowhere. A thin, bony, naked man, impossibly old. Blue electrical fire burst from points in his abdomen and upper thighs, crawling in Jacob's-ladder tendrils over his torso and limbs.

And the last thing Ani ever saw, through the flames and greasy smoke, was this apparition looking down upon him with his kindly, kindly eyes.

Parareality

In a place that had no name, a place indefinable in spatial terms or temporal terms, or the terms of organic life, something vast and inimical and unknowable watched our minuscule and stunted reality as it flickered and thrashed – though 'watched' cannot begin to encompass the full extent of its perception.

But human imagination must be expressed in human terms. 'Watched' will do.

It watched the throes of the world – and was aware upon some low level of its being that a certain organic

47

unit, a 'man', had been ripped violently from its proper place.

A small, almost imperceptible imperfection in the barriers between the worlds – but an imperfection that could be worked upon, teased apart. A point where the thing could sink its abstract jaws and feed.

It would be a mistake to believe that the eating of everything that exists in terms of organic life would be of more than idle interest to this thing, more than some idle snack.

But it wanted that snack.

Call it the Medusa.

INTERLUDE

Gagging for it (Cut-up Capers)

The Academy switchboard connects you right away with selected, very beautiful models who'd *love* to escort you. All educated, all friendly and fun. *The bi-sexual temp has the office staff hot and horny as she gets it over the typewriter, is molested in the lift and fornicates with the girls in the broom cupboard.* Alpine milkmaids, French students, Swedish au pairs, oriental dancers, latin beach girls, nurses and teachers . . . somehow or other I wriggled free and stumbled across the stile – only to see Jan flat on her back with her legs spread. *A young family friend visits and he's randy. He does not object and soon she has her tits out, and then she's naked and they're at it all over the house.* She was pissed out of her brains, and giggling like a complete idiot. As soon as the lads saw her the dreaded 'Gang-bang!' chant went up, and soon we both of us were being shafted this way and that by just about anyone who was game enough to drop his pants and perform in front of his mates. (Not many said no, I can tell you!) It was what you might call a bawdy day out, but a bloody good time was had by all! None of the lads thought badly of me and Jan for misbehaving, and we're all really looking foward to our next day at the races! *Dressed in black leather, she watches her friend and husband at it while she plays with a big black dildo*. I'm 21 years old and I can't get enough. If live conversation is what you want, I will talk to you for as long as you need, and as dirty as you feel! Just ring me and I will turn you on! This is a real conversation. Credit cards accepted. LESBIAN SECRETS – EXPOSED: the truth revealed by Debbie Dyke! LESBIAN ADMISSIONS: dare you listen? LESBIAN LETTERS read by Dillis Dial 'O': what you've always wanted to know – and hear! LESBIAN ADVICE CENTRE: just listen to the tape-recorded message on this sensitive subject.

'Pornography,' Andrea Dworkin tells us in *Letters from a War Zone*, 'is not a genre of expression separate and different from the rest of life; it is a genre of expression fully in harmony with any culture in which it flourishes . . . One looks at the pages or the pictures and one knows; this is what men want and this is what men have and this is what men will not give up.'

Two men forced a pretty schoolgirl to watch a blue movie while they raped her, a court heard yesterday. And they acted out the porno video scenes flickering on the screen, said Mr Roger Scott, prosecuting. 'They practised on her what they were seeing.'

– *Daily Star*

SLICE TWO

A New State of Being

The Big House

No one came to the house now. Sometimes Lucy Too thought she heard voices in the walls, saw whispering insubstantial shapes like ghosts, but no one actually came.

There had been a little girl once: pale and twitchy and aggressive and acting as though she owned the place. Lucy Too hadn't liked her much.

She had been here for a *long* time now. She had no way of telling time but sometimes, in her dreams, she remembered a world full of lights that she could *fly* through, a world so incompatible with the house that she could not imagine it now. She never found the way back.

Now she prowled, catlike, through the passages and stairwells and plaster crumbling to expose the lath; a thin pale girl in leather and iron, lit by dim and guttering lamps.

For a while she lay in the long grass of the mammal garden, listening to the monkeys screaming in the twilight jungle outside. Then she went up to the people stacks and infested Little Princess, parading in front of a mirror with a cup and ball before tiring of it.

Then she spent some time watching the Bloody Woman. It was quite restful, really. Like a waterfall.

After that, she went to the libraries in the east wing and just read for a while. Everyone should read, she thought; you learn a lot of interesting things.

And then the house began to shake. Something clawing, cutting at the bedrock, a hollow booming and hammering at the foundations. A heavy book bound in red morocco and encrusted with agates toppled from its lectern and hit oak boards with a thump and a spray of dust.

Wherever you went there was a secret door. The house was like that. Lucy Too pulled back a section of bookcase to reveal a circular and faintly glowing tunnel, its walls fleshy like oiled skin.

A rumbling from below. Lucy Too went down. Down the stairwell. Down the Stem.

Down to the core.

Psi Division, MC1

There was no sense of transition: she was simply *there*. Lying on her back on something soft, light shining diffuse and red through her eyelids.

Karyn opened gummy eyes and blinked, gazed up into the overhead fluorescents. Every muscle was relaxed and curiously numb. It was not that she was unaware of the input from her nerves, not that she was unable to perform motor-functions, but that she could not *feel* them. This, for example, was a hand

52

she could control via musculature and neural systems rather than *her* hand.

This was the result of the suppressants, she knew, remembering the sensation from a time in Rookie training when she had misjudged a self-administered dose.

She was aware that padded polymer straps secured her forearms and calves, but had no desire to move or act in any way. She simply lay there – automatic processes keeping respiratory and systolic and digestive functions operating, higher functions operating on the same level . . . until the straps snapped back and a helmeted face loomed across her field of vision.

'Just what the drokk's going on here, Karyn?' Sator said.

Officially, Psi Division was self-governing, led by a departmental head – currently one Psi Judge Shenker – in much the same way as any other division.

Unofficially however, given the general reputed instability of psychic talents, certain fail-safes were built into the system: a crack squad of Special Judicial Squad Judges, constantly monitoring the Psis, ready to step in to deal with any problem and, if necessary, certain individuals.

Sator was the leader of this squad: a hardcore Senior Judge of absolute ruthlessness and efficiency. He had no prejudice against genetic deviations *per se* – a bigot just waiting for the chance to land with both feet would be disastrous in such a position – but should the need arise he was capable of wiping out every single Psi in the city without compunction or regret.

'Half the drokking Psis are down,' he said grimly. 'And the low-graders are gibbering about migraines and fatigue, but they can't pin-point the cause.'

Karyn made her mouth move. 'What about Shenker? What about the bigtime precogs?'

'Total basket cases. We zonked them out and put them in stasis. All the heavy-duty people are out for the count.

'Something's making the Psi people crazy, Karyn – and it only seems to affect the areas of the brain specific to them. We've crash-engineered a batch of anti-suppressants to try and reactivate the normal human functions. You're the first one we could get talking. What the hell's happening?'

Karyn made her head turn, and saw the couches to one side of her, the unconscious figures strapped to them in their uniforms and coveralls. She was in the medicentre.

Had she been in her normal state, she would have simply been aware of where she was, and the people around her, without the need to use such basic devices as her muscles and eyes – and it was only now, now that her attention had been called to something missing rather than something actually there, that she realised the true extent by which her perceptions had been truncated. The flow of the world in which she had lived and breathed all her life was shut off from her: she was locked precisely within the space of her physical body.

This was an entirely new experience for her. She felt her brain activating the reflexes of fear.

Was this, she wondered, what Norms felt like all the time?

'I . . .' Karyn checked herself over – and it was

54

like running the diagnostics on a cyber-system, utterly mechanistic.

'There's nothing outside,' she tried to explain. 'It's the drugs. I don't live there now, and I can't tell you what's happening out there because I don't *live* there anymore.'

Sator snorted. 'I should have known. We got a choice between a roomful of cabbages and a bunch of walking zombies like you. Some choice.'

Something there. Some connection in the basic thought processes that Karyn was unused to thinking in.

'What were the symptoms?' she asked Sator.

The SJS man shrugged. 'Personality fragmentation, screaming fits, incoherence,' he said. 'Lashing out in animal panic.'

Karyn thought-processed this. 'Nothing physical?'

Sator shook his head. 'No directly related physical damage. We had to be a little rough in subduing some of them. A couple of broken bones and internal injuries. A couple of guys were out in public when they flipped out. We had to take them down, one of them permanently. Nothing serious.'

The image of Moloch jerking and haemorrhaging flashed before her eyes. Karyn swung herself off the bed. 'Take me to Moloch.'

'You?' Sator tried to shove her back. 'You're going nowhere, girl. The only thing you people have going for you is your funny stuff – and without that you're nothing, you get me?'

Without thought-processing much about it, Karyn stuck a hand through the uniformed Judge's surprised attempts at self-defence, gripped him lightly by the scruff of the neck and put her face close to his.

'Listen, Sator,' she said. 'I might not be able to do that funny stuff for a while, but I know more about it than you can shake a stick at. Plus I reckon I'm more of a Judge firing on two cylinders than you are on all six. Do you want to risk it?'

Sector 8 (Chakra Puja), MC1

'We can patch up the soft tissues,' the Med-Judge said. 'Crash-graft muscle tissue and artificial tendon – but the bones are a different matter. Femur and patella and tibia shattered, ankle dislocated . . . you're going to need a week in regen, maybe more.'

'Drokk that,' Dredd said. 'Until I get direct orders from the Senior Judge, this is my show. You get me as mobile as you can as fast as you can.'

They were in a prefab field module, set up by the Shok-Tac forces Dredd had seen vectoring in for a landing at the point he lost consciousness through loss of blood. Through the translucent polymer of the cramped geodesic shell the dark shapes of transports manoeuvred lumberingly overhead. There was the roar of heavy-duty impellers and the faint sound of shouted orders as forces deployed themselves.

Dredd was on a field couch, left leg enclosed by a med-pak as its micromanipulators sliced and grafted implants into his tissues.

The Med-Judge thought about it. 'I can give you some endoskeletal support,' she said. 'Effectively it's a glorified leg-brace with microservo assist. Just don't expect more than seventy, seventy-five per cent effectivenesss is all.'

'It'll do.' Dredd switched in his mike again and

called up Justice Department Control. 'Anything new happening here?'

'You got all we have, Dredd,' the voice of Control said. *'The demolition charges sealed Chakra Puja Block from ground assault, one thirty-second call to Justice Central telling us they have hostages and they're not afraid to use them and that's it. Heavy assault weaponry and Grud alone knows what else. They're sitting tight.'*

The med-Judge retracted the pack: the bruised and ruptured flesh of the leg had been opened and resealed and surgical-stapled, polymer derma-netting sunk into the livid skin. The Med-Judge raised him on the couch and strapped on the exo-struts, shooting inert bolts directly into his pelvic girdle to fix them.

'Move your toes,' she said.

Dredd moved his toes. The Med-Judge nodded absently and made a note on her hand-held. 'Remember this is only makeshift. If the extremities go numb, you get assistance pretty damn pronto before they go green and drop off, you get me?'

Back in uniform and hobbling slightly, Dredd left the geodesic and headed for the siege command station, a tangle of monitoring and communications equipment strung from a mobile framework and safely behind the cover of the deflection plates the transports had dropped around the block on arrival.

Forward of this, snipers trained their rifles up at Chakra Puja Block in the hope of a lucky shot. Off to one side stood the bulk of an armoured Shok-Tac Manta, powered up and on stand-by.

'Chakra Puja's filed as the Earth residence of the

57

"Unending Devotiates of Kloi Kloi Seki,' Control said. *'Out-system origin. The Neon Stars.'*

'I remember something about that,' Dredd said. 'Something about some hermaphrodite world-god being eaten alive by its thousand young, right?'

'That's what it comes out as. Apparently the real concepts are inexpressible in any human terms whatsoever. The earth-based religion's simply a bastardised form of the peripheral stuff, founded by one Menko Waco-Hyde for tax-and-info exemption purposes. It's basically just a luxury hab-complex for the rich.'

'So why would they barricade themselves in and start blowing people to drokk?' Dredd said thoughtfully. 'This is the work of fanatics – and no way do a bunch of fat bastards looking for a tax break fit the profile.'

He had reached the command station. 'No communications going out or in,' one of the Tek-Judges manning it said. 'They pulled the plug on almost every phone in the entire block after they made the call. Those we can access on override just show blank walls.'

'Motion detectors?' Dredd said.

The Tek-Judge indicated blips on a monitor. 'A lot of people in defensive positions, a large concentration in the middle of Level 17, another looser grouping on 16. Only nine hundred fifty to a thousand moving bodies in all.'

'And this place was built for fifteen thousand.' Dredd scowled. 'This smells like paramilitary incursion and clean-up.' He studied the outputs from vid-cams scanning the street before the block, indicated a charred and impact-twisted body – one of the gunmen who had been blown through the Chakra

58

Puju windows before the bombs went off. 'Send a drone out to run some IDs. Do it slow. These drokkers aren't going anywhere, and there's no point in going overt until we take them down.'

Brit-Cit

In Brit-Cit Zone Zero, in his plush and opulent offices in the New Old Bailey, Senior Judge Warner, a sub-controller of the Brit-Cit CID, watched a newscast with a cold and growing sense of terror.

From the holo-solid the spotlit face of Dawn Farren of DataDay News beamed from a night-time street with the foxy, triumphant satisfaction of a reporter with a scoop. A flashing overlay in the corner read: LIVE.

'. . . hour ago,' Dawn Farren of DataDay News was saying, 'we received notification from a pressure group calling themselves the Albion Liberation Army, detailing a cannibalistic practice so repugnant that the full details cannot be revealed on this channel. A full report is available to AdultNet subscribers with appropriate smartcards.

'In their call, the ALA offered us the location of where the perpetrators of these acts are currently restrained, and the promise that Justice Department forces would not be notified until we were on air and . . . and yes: here they come now.'

The camera tracked from Farren and zeroed in on a section of garbage-strewn sidestreet, in which a number of human forms lay piled: dead or unconscious, it was impossible to tell.

A Justice Department transport racked itself down on its hydraulics. Uniformed Judges disembarked and began, rather self-consciously, to load bodies into the back.

The process took five minutes, during which the camera was able to zoom clearly in on a number of faces. Then the camera tracked back to Farren.

'As a condition of this information,' she said, 'the ALA demanded that certain key names connected with this obscenity be made public . . .'

A display appeared to one side. Text crawled up it.

The vid-phone on Warner's desk bleeped. The screen remained blank, the external speaker silent. He picked up the handset, held it to his ear and listened for a full minute.

'Yes,' he said at last, nodding automatically in the way that people do even when there is no one there to see. 'Yes, of course I know. It's his style. That Albion Liberation Army reference was like sticking up a couple of fingers. I understand.'

Sector 8 (Chakra Puja), MC1

The drone wound its way through the deflection panels and shields and trundled for the blackened corpse. In the windows of the block above, shapes flickered but no target exposed itself for the snipers.

The drone reached the body and extended its manipulators. In the command-station, monitors flickered as it relayed visual and DNA data.

'Run them through Central,' Dredd said. 'Concentrate on names connected with extreme religious cults, then widen to terrorist, then general.'

The response was almost instantaneous.

'Raco Elwood Katchor,' the voice of Control said.

60

*'Two years cube-time, four years psycho. Affiliations
with a string of crazies over the last ten years – last
known affiliation a bunch of charmers calling themselves the Votives of the New Dawn. We're cross-
reffing now: leader of the cult is one Absolom Leviticus Thead.'*

Chakra Puja, MC1

The chapel stank of fear and confinement. Nothing
tangible had changed – the Faithful had, after all,
occupied the Chakra Puja for two months with no
thought of leaving. It was merely the knowledge that
they were trapped, that there was now no way out.
Ripples of frightened murmuring ran through the
crowd, building in intensity. Oven-like heat and lack
of sleep, a feverish and paranoid pressure that, at
some point, must surely crack into mass panic.

Absolom Leviticus Thead walked through those
of whom he was the absolute Master: a huge man,
seemingly sculpted from solid muscle, wrapped in
his rough hessian robing, unadorned. His face was
wooden, incapable of expression, a cypher only
capable of making such movements as, say, opening
and closing the slit of his mouth when he spoke.

Ah, but his eyes . . .

His eyes were those of a medieval saint: calm and
clear and filled with an unending love. They were
the eyes of a psychopath.

As he moved from group to group, occasionally
brushing a head with his hand, they looked up at
him with blind adoration and joy – the basic, automatic responses he had instilled into each of his
Faithful from the beginning. But underneath, on

61

some deeper level of which they were themselves unaware, he saw the terror and knew that at any moment the terror could turn to hate.

Something must be done now.

Absolom Leviticus Thead made his way to the dais. He stood before his children, his arms outstretched, and the murmurs lapsed into silence.

In calm, precise tones that rang around the chamber, the Master began to speak.

The Big House

The pit of the Stem was vastly wide, impossibly deep, walled with red and fractured crumbling brick, vine-like vegetation clinging and trailing.

Twisted iron stairways and catwalks wound down, giving access to dark openings and doorways, lots of them. Lamps and burning torches respectively hung and protruded from the walls, limning the forms of gargoyles, incomplete sculpture, fragments of mosaic.

The depths of the Stem were obscured by grey mist. Here and there the dart and flutter of unidentifiable flying creatures.

Lucy Too went down, clinging precariously to the rail.

It took a long time. The steps and the catwalks became vestigial, fractured easily, fell apart at the touch. More than once she was forced to fling herself across the gaps where they had given way completely.

Through the mists and through the dark, listening to the things chittering and crawling in the dark.

And, at length, the bottom of the pit. Cold, sourceless light like moonlight illuminated the flat and sandy plain stretching from the wall, the eroded humps and crags of ancient rock formations. Nothing lived down here, now. Nothing was contained. There were no secondary functions.

Like music or like abstract art, the form defined the function, the structure was the meaning. This was where the house was nothing but itself. Unchanging.

Immutable.

And still the hammering and roaring. The ground hummed and vibrated under her feet.

And then the sand began to shift. Slowly at first, just a few grains stirred by some nonexistent wind, then faster.

The sand parted to reveal the bedrock, and with a deafening *Raak!* the bedrock split open.

And then Lucy Too was running back, running for dear life. Behind her, magnesium light flared from the rift and dark shapes moved within.

The Undercity, MC1

Suspended from the black brick sewer roof by a length of slimy chain, a globe of frosted glass swayed minutely; perpetual, variegated firefly-light flickering and pulsing, lost in the black of the walls at each apogee.

The light, when it illuminated, illuminated an islet of accumulated human waste, around which the trickle of the sewerstream flowed, upon which squatted the thin, albino, wasted figure of a man, watching the ripples and whorls appearing in the mercury-like substance filling the dish he held before him in his clawed and arthritic hands – moving, this liquid, seemingly of its own accord.

The wasted man was ancient before his time, whatever that time might have actually been. Muscles and tendons had atrophied over the course of years if not decades, the joints calcified, skin tissue-thin and long since split at the joints to expose them. The man was completely immobile now, could only listen to the distant, whispering, seductive voices, the slither and crashing and thrashing of reptilian creatures. Physical requirements were taken care of by way of wide rubber tubes inserted into throat and colon, and periodically replaced when they rotted.

The wasted man had not moved in more than two years – and only then to topple over due to some explosive concussion from the new city above the old city over the sewers. He had been promptly righted by the girl who fed him and cleaned him, who replenished the stuff in his bowl and would replace him when the time came for him to die. As was the way.

The after-images detonated black and purple behind his eyes and a wave of power coursed through him, distending his arteries and veins and lymph ducts, igniting the vestigial oil in his pores with brief, pin-point flashes. The scrying-bowl fell from him, skin and glutea sloughing with it to land in a hiss and sputter before him.

Absently, the wasted man contemplated his burning skin and waited. Waited for the girl. He had something to tell her.

'What?' Treasure Steel realised she had slipped into a semi-stupor. She shook her head sharply to clear it and took another pull on her botulism in a bottle – she had acquired a taste for real beer from Armitage and, she knew, she was drinking far too much of it of late. 'Do what?'

'It was all over the holo,' Arna repeated. 'They called *DataDay* first, and they were on hand so even the Judges couldn't cover it up.'

'Oh. Yeah,' Treasure said. 'Right.'

'What do you think?,' Arna asked her. 'Do you have any idea who these ALA people are?'

Arna was maybe twenty years older than Treasure, and Treasure had known her since her first, faltering steps on the scene – had indeed been helped and guided by her through the rough initial stages. Small and slight and utterly compassionate, Arna exuded an innate sense of motherliness, and, without a shred of predation, tended to attract the younger women who were coming to terms with their nature.

She was the most capable and level-headed woman Treasure had ever known, had been her first real lover and even now, three years later, Treasure regarded her as one of the closest of the people she loved, second only to the woman she had married. And when she looked into her calm and steady eyes, she knew that Arna *knew*.

'We don't have clue one,' she said. 'We probably never will.'

'It doesn't matter,' Karli, who was Arna's latest

protégé, said. 'None of it matters. It's just more of the same old boys' games.'

Sixteen and baby-butch, Treasure thought: eyes alight with the self-conscious fervour of the recent convert – who has suddenly found some all-encompassing, automatic thought-system that will make her right forever, without ever actually having to think for herself ever again. Treasure's first reaction upon meeting her was: *Where the hell does Arna dig them up from?* Followed closely by: *Was I ever like that? Was that ever me?*

Karli, it seemed, was predatory in spades. Treasure had so far twice been forced to remove a surreptitious hand that had landed on her thigh and travelled up. She did so again as Karli warmed to her theme.

'These ALA of yours are just another bunch of big men playing hero – and even if they were women it would be just as bad. Worse. They'd be actively supporting a patriarchal, sexist . . .'

Oh dear Grud, Treasure thought. She's going to say *hegemony* in a minute and when she says it I'm going to kill somebody.

She finished off her beer and scanned the interior of the club. Happy, boisterous people on the dance-floor, two slim and somewhat cloney men she vaguely knew performing a laughing, exaggerated and expertly choreographed mock-fight through the strobes and other dancers.

In the soft-lit drinking area, a muscular leatherboy she remembered with affection from her brief and highly enjoyable if ultimately experimental bi phase, chatted amiably with a couple of SM dykes. They caught her eyes on them and raised their glasses to her with smiles.

The muted holos were switched to InterNews: a chaos of Judges and vehicles around a partially damaged block crawling with bas-relief alien creatures. An overlay said the image was live from Mega-City One.

Terry, who some minutes before had gone to the bar to get more drinks, had been waylaid by Juna, an old-time TV in all her regal glory, and was involved in an animated conversation. No hope of sudden rescue from that quarter, then.

'. . . so you can't use terms like "blame". That's just another part of the guilt-trip they try to lay on us. What you have to remember is that these women have . . .' Karli was now elaborating upon a rather baroque argument to the effect that the women taken down in the Tight White bust, by way of being women, could not be held accountable for their actions.

Treasure remembered the clean-up after they had dealt with the security, when between them she and Armitage had restrained and sedated the proprietors and clientele before checking out the kitchens and the back rooms: the faces of the women who had supplied the raw product willingly, the faces of those who had *consumed* the product . . . She suddenly felt very tired and very old.

She saw that Karli, as she elaborated, was pulling something out of her repro 501s – and with a small start recognised the slim polyprop mass of a keesh inhaler. She shot a glance to a suddenly slightly nervous Arna.

'Don't make me do it,' she said in low tones.

'So,' Arna said loudly. 'It must be a little embarrassing for Judges like you, Treasure, these vigilantes doing your job. What with you being a Judge and all, Treasure.'

The inhaler disappeared very quickly. Karli looked at her sharply. 'You're a Judge? So of *course* you won't agree with me. You've already sold yourself out to – '

'Look, I'm sorry,' Treasure said. 'I really don't want to talk to you any more.'

It crushed the child – and suddenly Treasure saw that this was exactly what Karli was: feeling very small and insignificant, and trying to be brave, and desperate for the approval of the people that she loved.

What Treasure had dismissed as simple pipsqueaking PC obnoxiousness had been the first timid, clumsy attempts of a fledgling to spread her wings and fly – only to be slapped down with blank contempt. Treasure looked into Karli's suddenly mortified, stricken eyes and knew that in one instant she had shattered this child's new-found and entirely precarious sense of self-worth utterly.

But Treasure was all out of sympathy. She shoved herself up from the table. She hadn't been drinking that much, there was no way she could have drunk that much, but the table seemed to be covered with bottles. One or two of them toppled onto the floor.

Treasure staggered through the crowd to Terry and pulled her away from Juna with rather more force than she had actually intended. 'Get me a drink. Get me a drink now.'

Gingerly, Terry ran a hand over the bruises Treasure's fingers had left in her arm. She was in her early twenties, slim and blonde with pale green-grey eyes that Treasure had fallen in love with from the instant she had seen them. She was currently wearing a black stretch off-the-shoulder number, lipstick and jewellery and fem as all get-out save for a pair of hobnailed boots for the hell of it.

'What did you do that for?' she said angrily.

'You said you were getting me a drink and I want a drink.' Treasure was shouting now. 'You went away and said, I want, I you said . . .'

For some reason Terry had her arms round her. Delayed shock, probably, Treasure thought as she pressed her face into her partner's neck; pull yourself together, Treasure. Get a grip.

The images she had suppressed while logging off and heading home and dragging Terry out to get totally wrecked returned with a vengeance. It was not the hateful faces of the women who had supplied the product willingly. It was not the condition of the women who had been unwilling.

It was not, ultimately, even the nature of the product itself.

It had been the methods of preparation.

'It's okay,' Terry murmured as she stroked her. 'It's okay . . .'

Treasure lifted her head to look at her, bloodshot eyes agonised and full of self-loathing – if self-loathing can be extended to encompass an entire species.

'I want to go home,' she said in a small voice. 'Please. I want to go home.'

Sector 8 (Chakra Puja), MC1

'*Asolom Leviticus Thead,*' Control said. '*Brit-Cit national born twenty-seventy-three. Unremarkable education until the age of seventeen, when he squeaked into the Cambridge knowledge-factories majoring in psychology, pharmacology and comparative religious studies. Then his grades shot off the scale. Seems he found his vocation.*

'*On graduation he worked on psycho-PR for Brit-Cit MediCare – their public relations department's bigger than every other department put together, incidentally – before suffering some sort of collapse. Either paranoid schizophrenia, simple nervous exhaustion or tertiary syphilitic dementia. There's some dispute concerning the diagnosis.*

'*In 2110 he founded the Votives of the New Dawn in Brit-Cit. The impetus, apparently, was Necropolis here – the forces of darkness had made MC1 their own and he was determined to counter them with the forces of light.*

'*The religion itself was a total mish-mash: anything from Judaeo-Christianism to the dumber aspects of paganism to the World Ice Theory. Brit-Cit Justice Department observations at the time put the chances that Thead actually believed any of the garbage he was spouting at something less than four per cent. It was just the initial bait to lure the sad drokks into psycho-conditioning. By 2114 he had a flourishing cult of maybe seven thousand, before they were wiped out by the Gabriel attacks simultaneous to Judgement Day.*

'*Thead escaped. He resurfaced in Mega-City in 2115 – and all available data shows a vast psychologi-*

70

cal change. Maybe the horrors of Judgement Day triggered another collapse, maybe not, but it seems that he now believed his own creed absolutely.

'He was zealous, fanatical and utterly charismatic. In less then four months he gathered over five hundred followers before we landed with both feet and broke up the cult. Quite an achievement, given the number of home-grown crazies he was competing with. Thead was deported. Over the next few months his followers simply dropped out of sight.'

'So now they're back,' Dredd said grimly. 'They're back with a bang.' He considered the motion-blips on the monitors: five hundred cult-members and presumably as many hostages. Aside from those free-ranging in the block, there seemed to be two major groupings. The Level 16 group, moving less amongst themselves, was tentatively tagged as the hostages.

It might be possible, Dredd thought, to take out the cult by surgical strike and leave the hostages untouched – but a cult was not a terrorist group. By its very nature, a cult would contain innocents who had simply been conditioned to follow their master. And children. Taking out the Votives of the New Dawn *en masse* would be nothing more than butchery.

Now a number of blips were heading from the Level 16 group, towards what the floorplan overlays tagged as the stairwells.

'We're getting something through on the clamp-mikes,' a Tek-Judge said. She switched in a speaker. 'Voice ID matches Thead. He's giving them a pep-talk or something.'

Psi Division, MC1

After Moloch had been stabilised he had been left where he was: there had been no point in moving him. Flat on his back on the bed, saline and glucotics plugged into his nose, blood packs plugged into his arm. EEG leads trailed from his scalp to monitor-consoles. The read-outs were flat as a strap. On another monitor, pulse-rate blipped slow and steady.

With the hard-edged, crystalline clarity of her limited perceptions, Karyn took in the room: the smells of old sweat and fresh blood were discrete, identifiable odours without emotional weight; objects and their juxtapositions devoid of interest or interpretation as any Duchamp ready-made: a cloth doll cut open and stuffed with dried leaves, a pile of mucus-clotted tissues from some long-ago bout of grippe, papers scattered across a battered desk, amongst which a childish drawing of a house with a hundred windows, defaced in the lower quarter by an angry crayon scribble . . .

A Med-Judge was checking over the monitors. 'We patched up the physical damage,' he said, 'regenerated the damaged synaptic tissues. That destroys whole areas of memory, of course. He might be blank on a lot of stuff – but he should be *there* and responding.' The Med-Judge gestured towards the flat EEG readout. 'There's nothing. There's nothing inside.'

'So we access the hardware,' Karyn said. 'The meat machine.'

'And how do we do that?' Sator was getting impatient. 'Just on the off-chance you've forgotten

72

Karyn, every one of you funny people who might be capable of doing that is sort of indisposed.'

Karyn turned to look at him with her empty robot eyes. 'I wasn't talking about Psi techniques,' she said. 'I want to use the Think Tank.'

Chakra Puja, MC1

There was something wrong inside her head. She remembered Raan telling her, once, impatiently, just before he hit her to shut her up, that the brain had no internal sensation – but she could *feel* it. A physical sensation. Wire-worms squirming in her brain, radiating medusa-like, eating twisted tunnels through her mind.

And finding blocks.

And eating through them.

Desperately, Sela scrabbled through her head, trying to snatch at memories once so simple and easy to remember: a bogtown childhood; a life homeless on the pedways after her mother and baby sister died; letting a black market trader have her four-teen-year-old body in return for a bag of kelp scraps; the four years in the juve-cubes before she met Raan and ran with his gang; giving birth to Kelli and leaving him outside for a day and a night to live or die in accordance with gang ritual; seeing the Master for the first time and hearing him speak . . .

The memories were intangible, somehow unreal. Swathes of information cut through them; incident and association impacting and interacting, vast and chaotic and of impossible complexity.

It was like living in a cell for all your life: a bed and a toilet bowl and food fed through a slot. You

73

have everything necessary to maintain a small, cramped life; you have everything you need . . . and then, one day, you suddenly notice a hole in the wall you have somehow never seen before.

And through the hole an endless chamber full of suns.

Something inside her. Something inside. She could almost feel the shape of it.

On the dais, the Master stood with arms upraised. A number of Principalities stood on either side – although, Sela saw, Raan and several others were missing.

'We are living in the Last Days,' the Master was saying. He spoke calmly. He had no need of raising his voice. 'Oh, this corporeal world will continue for a while yet on its spinning course into the sun . . . but, oh, the world is dark.

'The forces of Darkness have surrounded us. They are here to pull us down like unto a wolf in the fold. They will extinguish the Light and Hope of the World.'

He's pulling all the triggers, Sela thought. *All of them*. She had no idea why she thought that.

The Faithful, with the exception of those too young to understand, now stood bolt upright, the eyes of every man and woman and child turned to the dais.

'We have suffered the Unbelievers to live,' the Master was saying. 'And they have summoned their foul minions to *destroy* us.

'But we are cleverer and more brilliant.'

He made a vague, fluttering gesture with his hand. From a doorway to one side of the dais a number of Unbelievers, maybe fifty in all, were herded into the chapel by Principalities with shockrods. They were

74

dazed and uncomprehending, stumbling vaguely against each other. Sela saw Raan, who was chivvying the last of them in, club a wasted and middle-aged woman to the floor.

A low growl of hatred formed in the five hundred throats of the Faithful.

'Do you see them?' the Master cried. 'Do you *see*? This is the filth we have allowed to live in our midst, whom we have succoured as our own and, oh . . . but oh, they have betrayed us.'

The growl became a roar.

'We have suffered them to live, but now no more. No more. *Smite* them, my children. Smite them hip and thigh!'

And the roar became an ululating scream.

And, as one, the massed ranks of the Faithful surged forward.

Brit-Cit

Terry held Treasure's head while she threw up and half-supported, half-dragged her to the car: an elderly and battered Saab originally designed to run on wheels. Treasure had found it in a Sector 4 junkyard and had spent a couple of months of off-duty weekends, renovating the rusting shell and converting it for impellers.

Terry, who made her living as an installation artist (*'A trifle jejune, but the sheer weight of commitment makes this a woman to watch.'* Quanta), had spray-bombed it with various fluorescents, recreated *Rainy Taxi* (Salvador Dali, 1938) in the interior and christened it Og, for the simple reason that it looked like one.

'Do you want to talk about it?' she said as she floated the car up on its impellers and swung out into the street. 'I know you always get pissed and belligerent when you're hurt, but I've never seen you this bad.'

'I . . .' Treasure tried to put what she was feeling into general terms: there was no point in burdening Terry with specific secrets that might endanger her. 'It's just that I saw some things I couldn't . . .'

'Listen, matey,' Terry said. 'I occasionally let the holo-vid pollute my Ka and you're not fooling me for a minute. They seek 'em here, they seek 'em there . . .'

Treasure was chagrined. 'Am I that obvious? *Car*?'

'K-A. Egyptian soul, y'know? Only to the people who love you.' Terry hit the Inner Orbital and switched to the lane that would take them home to Sector 3.

'We were having fun,' Treasure said. 'It was all a sort of joke. And then I saw these little . . . how can people *do* things like this?'

'Well you know my world as sex-killer theory,' Terry said. 'Man, woman or child, the world screws you, and when it's had enough of screwing you it kills you. We're all of us wounded and alone, lost and alone and screaming in the dark . . .'

'. . . but, still, you got to laugh, eh?' Treasure finished what had become a ritual joke between them and smiled despite herself.

'Yeah, but sometimes we find people to cling to for a while. I'm being serious now. Miracles happen. Miracles happen all the time and most of them are other people.'

'Here,' Treasure said. 'You trying to get inside my

76

keks or what?' I could go for this woman, she thought.

She settled back in her seat ≢nd let herself relax, losing herself in the hypnotic flow of the lights through the polyplex canopy, the lights in the rear-view mirror.

After a while she said, 'Terry?'

'Mm?' Terry was concentrating on her driving.

'Can you take the next exit ramp? I need to check something out. I think we're being followed.'

Sector 8 (Chakra Puja), MC1

In the command station 'alert-systems were throwing small but persistent transputronic fits.

'He's set them on the rampage, Dredd,' the Tek-Judge said. 'They're killing the hostages.'

'So we take them now and we take them hard,' Dredd growled. 'It's their body-resyk ritual. Standard Shok-Tac assault and support. Get those fliers in the air *now*.'

The Tek-Judges ran the scramble sequence. The whine of impellers from the Shok-Tac transports on stand-by accelerated to a throbbing roar.

Dredd glanced briefly to the console on which he had been studying the Chakra Puja floorplans. 'Tag one of the reserve squads to my personal command. I might just have an idea.'

Psi Division, MC1

The development of true Artificial Intelligence technology had been hamstrung from the start by the mechanistic approach of Turing and his successors, who had mapped their theories and neuroses onto the world rather than vice versa, who had seen human intelligence as algorithmic when it was in fact holistic.

It was only with the sufficient refinement of holography that a new approach became evident – the generation or replication of a structure in its entirety, as opposed to a step-system emulating that structure's apparent function.

The Think Tank was a glorified three-dimensional holo-projector of such a high resolution that it operated upon the sub-atomic level – the level, it seemed, that true consciousness operated on. The brain of a subject was ultrasonically scanned and mapped onto the tank as a stable system, and then destabilised. Output from the resulting construct was routed via a transputer to a monitor, and by way of sophisticated imaging software could reproduce the thoughts and responses of the original subject almost exactly.

The only drawback was that the unstable construct was subject to accelerated decay, and had a life-expectancy of less than an hour.

The Tek plugged the Think Tank unit into the ultrasound coils wrapped around Moloch's head and ran the download routines. Vaguely, Karyn expected some sort of menacing and accelerating hum, but there was no sound.

The process was instantaneous. On the monitor, through the wash of static, a flickering and hideously distorted face screamed.

'*Mouth!*' the console speaker shrieked. '*Mouth! Mouth! Mouth! Mouth! Mouth!*'

The Tek turned down the gain and scanned her

read-outs, typed rapidly on her keyboard. 'I'm shutting down the areas affected by the disruption.'

The drugs Karyn had been pumped with were beginning to wear off. She could feel her inner self slowly expanding – and she could feel the howling chaos that threatened to drive her mad. She took a suppressant from her belt pouch and dry-swallowed it.

'Won't that just make him like I am now?' she said.

The Tek shook her head. 'This is micro-specific. We can fine-tune it to a higher level than the drugs.'

On the monitor, the face of Moloch sprang into focus. Karyn noted that Moloch's self-image tended more towards the romantically consumptive, somewhat like the faces in an Aubrey Beardsley drawing, than the seedy and slightly ratty original.

'Hi, Karyn,' the image said, user-friendly imaging routines tracking the pupils of his eyes to her face. 'What's happening? I can't move. Why can't I move?'

Karyn glanced briefly to Sator, who stood by the door poker-faced. He shrugged. Karyn turned back to the screen. 'You're, ah . . . actually you're in the Think Tank.'

'What?' The face of Moloch dissolved into panic-stricken rage. You mean I've got, what, forty-five, fifty minutes tops before I bite the big one? You drokking *bitch*!'

'They always do that,' the Tek said, typing frantically.

Abruptly, the face of Moloch was calm. 'Suddenly I feel pretty relaxed about it. Okay. If you've got me

79

in the Think Tank then you must want to talk to me pretty badly. What do you want to talk about?'

Brit-Cit, Sector 3

In his Sector 3 conapt, Detective Judge Armitage lay sprawled on the sofa with his feet up, flicking absently through a battered soft-bound book of litho plates: Duchamps's *Bicycle Wheel* and *Chocolate Grinder 2* and *Bride*, Richter and Janco and Segal, *The Rope Dancer Accompanies Herself with Her Shadows*, *Tu M'*, *Egg Board* and *L'Enfant Carburateur* . . .

His cheeks itched from shaving off his muttonchop whiskers. In the shower he had caught himself on the point of neurotically scrubbing himself clean over and over again as though to wash the filth off him, and had sternly controlled himself.

In a domed monitor fixed to the ceiling of the room, a diffuse and reddish glow somehow managed to suggest angry inactivation, which 'Taea, Armitage's home-AI system had lapsed into after he had cordially invited her to shut up and piss off.

When they had logged off, Treasure Steel had told him she fully intended to grab hold of her spouse and go out and get pissed for a week, and had invited him along. Steel, he knew, had not quite yet learnt to let the rougher aspects of the job roll off her back; Armitage had seen the trauma in her eyes – had found himself strangely touched and flattered that she felt close enough to him to include him in her cleansing process – but knew that the last thing she needed was her superior officer hanging around while she went through it. She needed to be with the people she loved.

But now, left to his own devices, the Detective Judge found himself regretting that he had declined the offer. For some reason the events of this particular day had disturbed him deeply. He took another pull on a half-pint bottle of what was effectively pure ethanol and which had been full a couple of hours before.

It was not, he reflected, as if he hadn't seen worse in his time, either on the force or before. He had, after all, during the Civil War, been one of the first people into Gabriel's DeathZone, had seen the remains of the entire population of Birmingham vivisected and strung through the streets. And before that, the squalor and brutality of the EMG-Zone, when he had been a member of the London Liberation Army and he –

A dead blank area of memory. The thought slid away from him before he could identify it.

It was not the actual events and images of the day. It was something else.

Intangible and in the back of his head, somewhere on the absolute periphery of mental line-of-sight, something was skewed and chaotic with the world. It was faint and almost imperceptible, but it was enough to tip him slightly off-balance, to destabilise him.

Something was bleeping in the tunic he had discarded when he had come home. His radio. Armitage realised that, without thinking much about it, he had been playing with his black-market gun for the last half an hour, looking down the snout with one eye and experimentally testing the pull on the trigger. He had, quite simply, no idea that he was doing it. He was rather grateful that he had remembered to unload the gun.

In the monitor on the ceiling, the manga-face of 'Taea appeared with silent and unnoticed concern.

With the over-compensatory, absolute control of the truly drunk he swung himself off the couch and pulled the radio from the tunic.

'Armitage!' Desperate, barely controlled hysteria. Treasure Steel. 'I'm home. We were followed *home*. I thought I could . . . but they were *waiting* for us. Terry's down and there's a *hole*. I think she's . . .' The voice devolved into choking sobs.

A muffled background voice, gunfire and then static.

Second phase disruptions

And in the vestigial undersea wreckage of the Lervantz-Steiger Penal Complex ('Aquatraz') a broodfemale birthed two-headed aquaphibian vampae.

And in Antarctica lights were seen deep within the ice.

And in the Cal-Hab Zone seventy thousand citizens simultaneously forgot three specific words.

And the bones of the world, the World Dragon, stirred.

Chakra Puja, MC1

In the Level 17 chapel, the Unbelievers desperately tried to back away – the relatively stronger and intact trampling the weaker – and found their retreat blocked by the bronze walls of the chamber. The illumination from the stained-glass window (a backlit leaded structure affixed to the wall rather than a window in any actual sense) cast slices of primary light across them as the Faithful fell upon them tooth and claw.

The Faithful tore them limb from limb. The Unbelievers squealed like pigs.

Kelli darted from Sela's side, wriggled his way through the press of the crowd eager for a piece of the slaughter, became lost from sight. Sela staggered unaware, all but insensate to the struggling crowd, the gouts of arterial blood jetting from its midst – images and memories exploding through her head, burning out the conditioned responses instilled by the Master's therapies, shattering the vacant, pliable, submissive automaton she had believed to be herself.

(*these are the basic statutes so you go through a door and you know what's in front of you anyway so* always *check the stuff on the you follow through with the elbow for a second strike and don't believe for one second you can*)

It was over in a matter of seconds. The mob rippled and howled as the Faithful cast about for something else to kill.

'There are more below,' the Master called from his dais. 'Hundreds more. Go below, my children, and bring them the *Light*!'

The crowd surged for the doors of the chamber.

A girl, barely in her mid-teens, eyes wide and blazing with fanaticism, lips pulled back from her teeth in a feral snarl, rebounded off Sela and knocked her flat. From somewhere outside came the rattle of rapid-fire and muffled detonations, the thrumming roar of heavy-duty impellers.

(*simple fact of living in and moving through the world accumulates stuff like that automatically such thing as a fair fight go for eyes and throat and balls where appropriate and go for them* hard *trinitrotoluene extends its kinetic energy at a rate of if you grease the outer surface of the jacket with simple household detergent it*)

And quietly, without a fuss, the last mental block came down.

And Sela, the real Sela, woke up.

Sector 8 (Chakra Puja), MC1

The Shok-Tac transports threw themselves into the air and streaked for the Chakra Puja, bracketed it in a triangular formation and hovered level with the seventeenth floor.

Electromagnetic grappling lines shot from the hatches, drawn by the carbon-steel supporting structure of the block, crunching solidly to the rockcrete outer surfaces with a small spray of alien statuary.

Shock-Tac troops spilled from the hatches, sliding down the wires on their harnesses with all guns blazing – only to be met by devastating, explosive rapid-fire in return.

It was a small miscalculation by Shok-Tac command – but catastrophic in effect. As the dead troops piled up on the wires they created a log-jam, those descending behind crashing into them and becoming sitting ducks.

And then the Soldiers of the Light played their, as it were, Final Trump.

Guided missiles streaked from the block, burst through the dead and wounded hanging Tacs with an explosion of meat and teflon-armour shrapnel, sidewindered to hit the transports.

Two of the transports went down like burning bricks. The third, crippled, flung its ruptured, twisted mass from the block, spilling human shapes from within, and lurched across the sky to hit a transit stack.

The figures in the Justice Department command centre devolved into frantic activity. Snipers opened up with covering fire as support-drones went through irregular concentric rings of blast shields and attempted to chop surviving troops from the wreckage of the transports.

In all this confusion, it was all but unnoticeable that several of the drones diverted towards the blasted, sealed-off lower levels of the block itself and began to dig.

Chakra Puja, MC1

Sela prowled Level 17, hearing the explosions and the gunfire outside, the roar as the Faithful took the hostages apart below, without thinking much about it.

And eventually she found one of the Soldiers of the Light patrolling the corridors.

He was, as it happened, the soldier she had encountered earlier that day. He was operating almost entirely on his conditioning now, scanning his surroundings and tracking his assault rifle smoothly like an industrial robot. Sela, presenting a distinctive image of one of the Faithful, would be relatively safe.

On the other hand, he might just be programmed to take out anything that moved.

Sela took the risk. She left the cover of an air conditioning unit and strolled calmly towards him.

'Get away from me, woman.' The soldier swung a hand to knock her out of the way.

And found his forearm in a vice-like grip. Two stiffened fingers of Sela's other hand lunged upwards, striking the exposed thin polymer where the body armour of the torso met that of the upper arm and punching through it, plunging into the nerve ganglion of the armpit and deadening the arm.

Angrily, the Soldier of the Light spun to face her – and caught the edge of her hand in the side of the head: the force applied with absolute precision to travel through the combat helmet and skull to concuss the brain within.

The soldier went down as though pole-axed. Sela spent a happy couple of minutes stripping him of weapons and other useful items and then, more or less as an afterthought, crushed his throat with her heel.

Psi Division, MC1

'We don't *live* there, you see,' the voice of Moloch said rather smugly. 'We don't live in this squeaky little three-dimensional world like old Pit-bull Features over there . . .'

'Yeah, well,' Sator growled from his position by the door. 'By my reckoning you're only going to be living full stop for another twenty-five minutes.'

'Thank you so much for reminding me. And in the same spirit might I offer the considered and reasonable response of: "Why don't you just eat stomm and die?"

'Consciousness is built into the universe on the quantum level, Karyn: integral to the very fabric of space-time. Atrophied drokks like Pit-bull Features can *perceive* time – but the Psis like us, who have evolved a certain degree of true consciousness, can actually *live* in it. That's how precognition and related phenomena work. Our apparent psychic talents are merely the first intimations of a world over and above our human perceptions and imaginings.

'We live in an expanded reality, Karyn. A *sur*reality – in the proper sense of the term and operating upon a higher order of connectivity. A polyfractal matrix produced by seven billion meat machines capable of referring to themselves.

'And now, I think, it's infested. Something's eating it.'

Chakra Puja, MC1

Those original inhabitants of Chakra Puja Block who still survived had been seperated into groups locked into chambers on Level 16. In one such chamber, originally a crèche for the younger, and still-working inhabitants with families, one Dudi Weeny pressed her ear to a now-filthy door painted with cheerful cartoon characters under the filth and listened to the crowd rampaging outside, listened to the screams of the dying.

Dudi Weeny had been one of those shark-like commodity brokers who had flourished in the decade after the Apocalypse War. She had joined the Devotiates of Kloi Kloi Seki and relocated to the Chakra Puja on the advice of her accountant. She lived almost entirely on her nerves, and had thus survived the starvation diet and the terror of the two months since the occupation more or less intact.

The other occupants of this chamber had not been so lucky: middle-aged and corpulent for the most part, originally filled with the bovine, mean-spirited complacency of the comfortably well-off, their skin now hung from their bones in folds and their sunken eyes shone with dulled upper-middle-class spite. They had not, one felt, paid out good money to be treated like *this*, and they fully intended to complain to the appropriate authorities.

A number of them had reverted somewhat and were surlily playing with the toys in the crèche. The chamber was smeared with human waste; the sanitary facilities intended to clean up after toddlers were long since clogged.

From her listening-post by the door, Dudi had heard the curt orders and the murmuring as the occupants of other chambers were led away. This was a part of the day-to-day ritual of the months since incarceration, and she had no idea of exactly what was happening to these prisoners, but she knew it wasn't anything good. At some point, she knew, the door would open and the guards would come for her.

This last time, so far as she could judge, the procedure had been different. More prisoners had been taken, and taken in another direction.

And then the roar of the mob.

Dudi Weeny listened to the screams and the brutal

sounds of killing, and knew that she was going to die.

Then the door slid open. Dudi Weeny lurched back with a cry of alarm as grey smoke wafted into the room.

A figure stepped through it: a woman in her early twenties, battered and wiry. Her head was shaved and she wore the slightly scorched remains of a hessian robe. An assault rifle hung from her shoulder by its strap, a handgun in her hands.

She glanced around the room with casual professionalism, then tossed a couple of keycards to Dudi, who caught them automatically.

'There's stuff going on down below,' she said. 'I don't have the time. Get as many of these doors open as you can, get as many people out as you can. I've set off a couple of haze grenades to increase the confusion – so just do the best you can, okay?'

With that, the woman turned and disappeared into the smoke.

It would, of course, be nice to record that this miraculous instant of reprieve awoke in Dudi Weeny some long-dormant nobility of spirit and concern for her fellow woman and man – that she followed the woman's instructions with presence of mind and courage, and distinguished herself by being instrumental in the saving of many of her fellow hostages who might otherwise have died.

It would, in fact, be nice to record that she did anything other than have it away on her toes with no thought but her own preservation.

But of course, she didn't.

Brit-Cit

Treasure Steel and her partner lived in a housing co-op on the fringes of Sector 3: originally converted from warehouse space to light-engineering modules for small business use, never actually occupied by small businesses and subsequently squatted. It had power and communications and was ideal for Terry's work, and the couple lived in a modified portable hab-capsule hanging to the back of her studio.

Armitage brought the car down heavily on the access platform, slewing it into a couple of derelict transporter shells raised on blocks with a crunch and a tinkle of glass.

He shot the doors and stumbled from the car, groping in the pocket of his trenchcoat for a battery-operated torch.

The beam tracked across the swingback doors until it hit a narrow access door set into them. The padlock was broken, hanging off its hasp.

Floorspace was not at a premium in the co-op. The studio was cavernous. Manipulator gear and half-tooled lumps of metal hung from chains. The hammering and groaning of pressed steel warehouse walls shifting in the wind. Something clockwork and hydraulic and vaguely insectoid towered off to one side, hooked to a gently humming charger, a dim blue light guttering within its structure, casting flickering cogwheel shadows across the walls.

'Steel?' Armitage staggered across the floor of the studio towards the steel-runged ladder leading up into the living quarters. His voice was slurred.

He blundered into an oxy-acetylene rig and fell flat on his face with a crash of pressurised canisters and an explosion of curses, before clambering his feet and pressing on with exaggerated care, muttering to himself with incoherent and drunken anger.

Such was his state that he totally failed to notice the dark figure as it emerged from the space between the living quarters and the floor of the studio, bringing up an automatic micro. Hollow-point slugs impacted in a tight grouping over his sternum and abdomen before he had time to react.

Psi Division, MC1

'I have a memory of expanding,' the face of Moloch said. 'It was perfectly natural. It was like wandering through the rooms of a house and making them your own . . .

'And then I sensed this presence – something vast and clawing and slithering in the back-brain. I only got impressions: something insectoid, wads of cancerflesh hanging from a wooden skeleton, slick leather stitched with twisted, oily gut . . . that's all pretty self-contradictory, I know, but I'm talking about impressions here, right?

'It was like . . . it wasn't like cybernetics. If you imagine inert organic substances like leather and rubber and the rest of it somehow imbued with life . . . like some vast AI transputer system, but mechanical, made entirely out of wooden cogs, but just the idea of it in my head and . . .'

Sator snorted with disgust. 'The drokking thing's raving.'

'Shut the drokk up,' Karyn told him absently. 'This is important.'

'. . . blank for a while there, but I remember this

91

sensation of being drawn towards it,' the face of Moloch was saying. 'Some abstract gravitation. I fell up into it and it began to cohere in my mind. I could feel the *shape* of it and – '

The screen went blank and silent.

'It's trying to access the areas we shut down,' the Tek-Judge said. 'Where he starts shouting "mouth" over and over again. I'll backtrack it.'

The Tek typed something into her console and the face of Moloch appeared again.

'What was I talking about?' he said.

'Nothing much,' said Karyn. 'Listen, Moloch. You remember saying that something was eating through this higher order of reality, disrupting time and affecting Psi functions . . .'

'Yeah. And just you wait till it eats down to the level that norms operate on. The world is *not* going to be a good place to be in.' The eyes of the simulacrum glanced to where the comatose body lay. 'I reckon I'm well out of it, wherever I am.'

Karyn made her voice level. 'But the other Psis just broke down mentally. How come you went into physical trauma?'

The simulacrum of Moloch looked smug. 'It's all a matter of degrees. I mean look at you and all the other Psis – hopped up and strung-out on so much junk it's a wonder you can talk and walk at the same time. That negated some of the effects. I was probably the cleanest guy on the force, so I got it full-strength, and even then I got it twisted.

'And that's what you really want to know, right? So let me tell you. You want to find where I'm gone, you're going to have to do it clean.'

The Undercity, MC1

The girl hauled herself out from the slick and cloying water and climbed the concrete steps, breathing heavily under the weight of the uncured ratskin bag slung across her shoulder. The bag contained a tarnished vacuum flask of some liquid substance that shifted uneasily within its containment as though it were alive, a stringy mash of fungus and rennet in a cotton sack, and a slim and exquisitely decorated knife wrapped in oilskin, its blade slick with half-crusted blood and cephalic fluid.

She had listened to what her father had told her, what she had to say. She knew it by heart. After the minute, crunching motions of the jaw had ended, after the desiccated whisper had subsided, she had sent him to his reward.

As was the way.

The girl came to the top of the steps, made her precarious way across a rusting catwalk to where a curious arrangement of rubber tubes and whistles were lashed makeshift to what might once have been an electrical intercom.

The girl removed a stopper from a tube and blew into it.

Chakra Puja, MC1

The demolition charges had been laid with precision, wrecking the lower levels without damaging the compressed carbon-steel supports that made up the geodesic skeleton of the block. The drones crawled upwards through the wreckage, cutting through solid

93

obstacles with their manipulators, hauling themselves up through open spaces on grappling lines.

On the second level they hit the layers of rockcrete and soundproofing that divided the commercial sections of the block from the residential, shot crampon bolts into the ceiling and crawled across it like inquisitive cybernetic flies until they found an access hatch.

The cargo hoppers opened and Dredd and his Shok-Tac squad hauled themselves up through the hatch.

They went through the maintenance ducts fast, hit Level Three and deployed themselves.

'Jovus . . .' Dredd glanced about himself. The Level Three corridor had remained untouched since the Chakra Puja's occupation. The walls were pitted with gunfire impacts, slathered with matter. Corrupt and bloated bodies lay where they had fallen. The larvae of insects, automatically zapped ultrasonically if they strayed from the Hinterland sector, squirmed.

Dredd leading the way, they headed for a stairwell. Dredd pulled his Lawgiver, stuck his head through the doorway – and racked it back sharply as explosive slugs richocheted and detonated.

He mentally replayed the image he had caught. Two figures in hi-impact body armour and ragged scraps of hessian on which were embroidered crude representations of burning torches, dug in one flight up behind an improvised emplacement of rockcrete blocks.

In less than a second he had factored the tactical variables. With two Tacs as a diversion it was doable. Shok-Tac troops were drawn from the iso-cubes, lobed and streamlined: they were expendable. Rap-

94

idly, he scanned his squad, deciding which to sacrifice.

It was at that point that gunfire sounded again from the stairwell: two shots, slightly muffled.

Then silence.

Dredd stuck his head through the doors again. The armoured figures lay slumped over the rockcrete blocks, heads blown off at the nape of the neck. A woman stood over them, of average size and wiry, an assault rifle slung from her shoulder, automatic in her hand.

Dredd brought up his own gun. 'Drop it. Do it slow. Do it *now*.'

'Hey, it's dropped.' Very carefully, the woman spread her arms and let the automatic hang from a finger by the trigger guard. 'It's okay. I'm Sela Kane. Deep cover. I'm Wally Squad, okay?'

The Undercity, MC1

In his cell the Duty Officer was at his devotions, turning the fragile pages of the System Support Manual, mouthing incomprehensible words, tracing diagrams of impossible complexity in the air. In a cage in one corner of the cell, an unhealthy, mangy chimpanzee stirred sullen and fitful. It had been marked with the sacred mutilation, skin flayed back from the five crucial points of its skull as per Standard Surgical Procedures.

Running from the walls and fixed to the dead remains of communications equipment were speaking tubes, each labelled with little pasteboard cards in the painstakingly neat hand of one copying the shapes of letters without the faintest idea of what they meant.

A crudely fashioned whistle-stopper of a tube gurgled and choked. The Duty Officer turned absently toward the sound, recognised the specific source and dropped his System Support Manual in shock. Startled, the chimpanzee chattered and scolded.

The whistle sounded again. There could be no mistake. Reverently he ran his finger along the pasteboard label: SEN SORSTATION THREE GRIDZERO.

The time had come. The time had come and he had lived to see it.

The time of Status Operational. The sleepers would awake. The giants would walk again.

His face alight with something like holy rapture, the Duty Officer broke the seals on the casket that had been handed to him after the ritual suicide of his father, gazed upon the small, thin, oblong talisman within, the runes etched into its surface: –

SPECIAL SERVICES Section 8

Phase two disruptions

And in the fetish-strewn streets of MexArcana an hallucinatory Coatlicue prowls through the poles and hanks of hair and feather, in her skirt of snakes and her necklace of hearts and severed hands and a skull. And in the Crystal Sector of Europa glass towers shatter as their occupants thrash in unison to a psychosomatic St Vitas' Dance. And in the Totalitarian Hegemony of Bangkok the spirit of Rati, Ragalata the vine of love, Kelikila the shameless, Mayarati the deceiver, appeared in her aspect of a huge-breasted woman to drive all who beheld her mad with carnal lust, without any noticeable difference.

And in the Trenches of Mega-City One, a killer burning with electrical fire is doing what he does best.

INTERLUDE

The Alternative Origin (A Missing File)

FOR YOUR EYES ONLY

To: Chief Judge Goodman, CenCom
From: DuPré, Emergency Hygenics Division
Date: 20–03–2072

Enclosed, transcripts of an item recovered from NYPD bunker 37 subsequent to Phase IV pacification. Said item appears to relate to an investigation by one Lieutenant Igor Waldkind ('Stanley'?) of a series of child murders.

Extant material is fragmentary at best. No date or actual location is legible, but internal references point to a date no later than 2007.

The item itself is laserprinted on A4 80 gsm stock, in an advanced state of decomposition due to excessive sulphite content. It appears to be the work of a technically literate but undisciplined and erratic personality – note the conversational asides.

Content is more or less self-explanatory. The list of names mentioned towards the end has not been found, which precludes hard correlation – but assuming that even a few individuals survived what appears to be a concerted programme of extermination by force or forces unknown, as an explanation for the remarkable similarities amongst the otherwise utterly disparate group of those exhibiting psychic talents, it is more than plausible.

It strikes me that this information could cause severe complications to the projected role of psychic talents in the Consolidation. I therefore suggest that it be suppressed. Bury it deep. And then seed the ground with salt.

– DuPré

FOR YOUR EYES ONLY

I'm going to print this out and then I'm going to wipe the disk and burn my notes and try to forget about this whole shitty mess. It probably won't matter, there's probably a superconductive rig locked onto my monitor even as I write, but it's the best I can do.

I don't like to think of myself as a coward, but this is just too

I've made up a guy in my head, called him Stanley — like the psychologist in that appalling multiple-personality book. (I mean, if that woman had 64 separate personalities and one of them was this literary genius on the level of Joyce, why didn't she get him *to write it rather than some schlock hack-writer who wouldn't know a gerund if it crawled up his, her, or their collective backside?) I'm going to write this to him so I don't let anything slip even by implication. That all right with you, Stanley?*

Federal systems were a total dead end. The clearance procedures were built into the hardware *when the Central Registry system was computerized: inte-*

100

gral to it. Any ID check tagged 'Special Services Section 8' comes up clean. No actual data involved.

No joy with NSA files either . . . so then I took off the time-lock, trawled through the dormant stuff, the projects that were shut down or never got off the ground . . .

There's some weird *shit in there, Stanley. Did you know that in the early '80s some bright spark proposed modifying the TV sets of certain visible left-wing militants to emit hard X-rays, killing them slowly with cancer? Those were the exact words used, 'killing them slowly with cancer'. The logistical problems proved too great and the project was put on hold.*

There's a lot of stuff like that, some of it going right back to 1945 and based upon accounts of death-camp experiments unearthed in the liberation – and some of those *files are cross-referenced right back to NSA. One-way windows, no trace of them on the other side. That's how I got in.*

I found it. Special Services Section 8 is inactive now, and even when it was *active, it was just a front for something else – something called the* Medusa Programme.

The Medusa Programme was set up some 27 years ago and ran for about ten, based in and operating from a series of disused sewers and tunnels running parallel to the Greater Metropolitan Subway. Plans enclosed. There are references to a 'bunker' of some kind, but I haven't been able to track it down definitely. I've marked the most likely locations on the map.

I also found specs for some heavy-duty data pro-

cessing equipment, optical technology years ahead of its time . . .

Who the Medusa Programme's controllers were, who its operatives were, I have no idea. I've found the skeletons of personnel files and salary scales and all the rest of it, but every specific detail has been erased.

They experimented on children, Stanley. They operated on kids. More than seven thousand of them over the course of ten years.

A number of doctors in the major cities across the US – names, again, erased – were given characteristics to look out for: a certain set to the features, a certain reaction to infra-red shone in baby eyes . . . and a lot of mothers were regretfully informed that their children had been stillborn. Older children just disappeared, ostensibly the victims of sex-related attacks. No bodies were ever found. Homeless children were just pulled in off the streets . . . but nobody was going to miss them, were they?

They did something to these children's heads. It gets confused here, but there seems to have been two basic procedures: hormonal treatment to enlarge and mutate the pineal gland, and cybernetic implants restructuring and directly linking the discrete sections of their brains.

Why, I have no idea. My first thought was that they were trying to make superminds or something – but all the evidence suggests that the children's minds were seriously disrupted. I disassembled one of the implants' operating systems and it seems to be some sort of autememe *generator: twisting incoming data into little self-referring personality constructs and mapping them onto the long-term memory . . .*

There's evidence to suggest that the children's DNA was disrupted too; re-engineered. I think that they were trying to make these modifications hereditary.

There are a lot of references to something called the 'Meld'. I think this was what the children were being prepared for, but I've no idea what it actually entails. Maybe the term was so basic that nobody bothered to define it.

The mortality rate was high; nearly two thousand children died during the operations. Those survivors old enough to be aware of the process were given post-hypnotic blocks, conditioned to forget that anything had ever happened to them. They were then distributed to various state-funded foster homes and adoption centres – and a lot of them just happened to end up in New York. Maybe some mothers even got their 'stillborn' children back. The children grew up and were able to lead more or less normal lives . . .

And that's the important point, Stanley. It struck me that these kids are now old enough to have kids of their own. *Enclosed, a partial list of couples those children ended up with. I ran a word-search on their surnames, using the names of your murdered girls . . .*

Your dead kids are the children of the Medusa Programme subjects.

I think somebody's trying to cover his tracks. Like I said, the background material goes back to the death-camps – and I have this godawful feeling that, like the death-camps, this wasn't done for any reason at all. It was just done because somebody could get away with it.

It hasn't ended, Stanley. The murders in the [location deliberately defaced from original source] *are*

103

*more noticeable because that's where the greatest
concentration of victims is, but what about the* rest *of
the country? The world?*

*This is too big for me. It's just too big. I said I
didn't like to think of myself as a coward, but I've
been lying awake, just wondering what people with
those sort of resources, people who are capable of
doing something like this, are capable of doing to
me . . .*

*You too, Stanley. Drop it. Leave it alone. Find a
rock or something and crawl under it and hide.*

*They're just going to kill and kill and keep on
killing, and you can try to pretend it isn't happening
or you can stand in their way and get squashed.
There's no* way *you're ever going to stop them.*

SLICE THREE

A Pocket Apocalypse

Psi Division, MC1

The sterile planes of the theatre, the archaic lines of the dialysis machine, triggered some long-buried memory in Karyn that the smooth modular lines and microsurgical packs of the contemporary Psi Division medibays never did. She remembered the time when, as a child, she had just started crying and crying and was unable to stop, when her distraught parents had taken her to the Sector Four clinic, and when her emergent psychic talents had been detected.

She remembered a dormitory painted a flaking snot-green. She remembered how, at night, through the walls, she heard people shouting things that didn't make any sense: that Hollowhead was there, Hollowhead was hanging off the *plate* . . .

There had been one woman in the ward, senile, who believed that she was still living in her own house, that the medics and orderlies were in fact her servants. She had been very old. There had been interesting bald, red, crusty patches in her wispy scalp.

The woman would shout at night how this was *her*

house, how it was a big, big house and how her servants wanted to kill her and slice her eyes. One night the curtains were drawn around the woman's bed, and the next day she was gone.

Her parents had come to see her. Karyn had asked, pointing to her mother's midriff, if that was her little sister. This had frightened them and they had gone away, and Karyn had never seen them again. Then a medic who insisted she call him Jerry, when his name was something entirely different, had explained that she was going to be a Judge.

The dialysis machine pumped blood through the hierarchies of osmotic membrane, filtering out the simple molecules of waste products and the complex strings of suppressants. Karyn lay back, staring at a junction between the ceiling tiles, immobile but for her breathing. A catheter dealt with the distilled water she had filled her stomach with. Regenerable microsurgical lesions had cut the nerves of her neck and armpits and groin to counteract any physical spasms that would ordinarily be dealt with by muscle relaxant.

The artificial contruct of Moloch had lasted another quarter of an hour, compensatory systems keeping it untroubled by its increasing fragmentation. The last coherent thing it said was: 'You know, I don't think human beings can survive without bodies. Embodiment is so much of what we are. If we didn't have them, I think we'd have to make them.'

The cleaning-out process had taken a couple of hours so far. Karyn had felt herself, her true self re-expand – and the chaos she had felt before expanded with it, hazing in her back-brain, a pressure like incipient migraine.

And there was something else. A raw and physical craving upon an entirely different level from the disruption. A mindless, animal urge to reach for the flap on her belt and . . .

'You bastitches!' she snarled to the Med-Judge watching over her. She realised that her teeth were chattering. The motor-neurons of her jaw and tongue and vocal chords had been left untouched so she could report any symptoms she was experiencing. 'The junk you give us is *addictive*, right?'

'That's, um, classified information,' the Med-Judge said.

With her perceptions restored, and now that this nasty thought had occurred to her, Karyn could have dug the information out of his head with little trouble – but what was the point?

Oh Jovus, she thought, no wonder Moloch always came across like he was about to go for your throat. Withdrawal symptoms – and all he did was cut down on the stuff as much as he could. How much would that account for his spasms during the disruption?

And what about me?

Her body felt far away and disassociated: some appendage on the extremities that had no real use, like the little toe of a Norm. Without really caring much about it she was aware of the taste of blood and a pain-reflex as she bit her tongue, that a hand was jamming in a mouth guard.

Psi Judge Karyn stared at the junction between four wall-tiles and expanded into the void.

Brit-Cit

Terry zipped through a streetmarket dead and dormant for the night and turned into a sidestreet. Treasure was kneeling on her seat, peering intently into the night. In her rear-view mirror, Terry saw the car behind them, low-slung and matt-black, barely distinguishable once noticed, and almost impossible to notice.

Terry had been crawlingly aware of its presence since her spouse had pointed it out: always there, never more than a car or two behind.

Now there was nothing between them.

'We're coming up on an intersection,' she told Treasure. 'The lights are changing. Looks like we're going to have to – '

'Don't you *dare*!' The sharpness in her spouse's voice shocked Terry, not least because of the sudden, horrified panic that lay beneath it. 'Stick your foot down. Do it *now*.'

Terry pressed the accelerator, hitting the interchange a couple of seconds after the lights changed. This late at night there were only a couple of cars that might have caused a problem and they didn't have time to build up much speed. She watched them spin lazily into each other in the rear-view.

'Is that going to lose it?' she asked.

'Not if it's what I think it is,' Treasure said grimly. She pulled the handset of her Department issue two-way from the dash and thumbed the switch. 'Dispatch? This is Mobile Tango Sierra one niner one. Do you copy?'

'We hear you,' the speaker crackled. 'This had better be important, Tango Sierra. We've got a city

108

eating the carpet here. Psi's down total, outbreaks of violent mania, mass hysteria running at . . .'

'My heart bleeds. Listen, Dispatch, I've got a tail and I think it's a stalker. I need some help here pretty damn pronto.'

'Yeah, I'll bet you do,' the voice said calmly. 'Good luck with it. All channels are jammed. Please hold. All channels are jammed. Please hold. All channels are . . .' This last from a voice-chip on a loop routine.

'Oh stomm . . .' Treasure said quietly. 'It's a heavy-duty hit. New Old Bailey's going to look the other way. The drokkers have given us up.'

Chakra Puja, MC1

Sela led Dredd and his squad up through the block. She had noted the positions of the Soldiers of the Light on the way down, and with the reawakened analytic processes of a Judge was able to identify them on Dredd's hand-held motion detector by their movements. They avoided them with only minor skirmishes.

'Thead doesn't know you're here yet,' Sela said as she refilled her ammunition pouch with clips from a soldier Dredd had blown away.

'How so?' Dredd said. He had intially been reluctant to trust Sela's advice, being of the opinion that years of deep cover might have eroded the qualities that a Judge was trained for – but since Sela currently had the only hard information as to what was happening in the Chakra Puja, he was forced to rely on her.

'Thead controls them utterly.' Sela glanced around

at the squad. 'Not like Shok-Tac. Justice Department conditioning and implants don't go anywhere near as deep. The Soldiers of the Light are utterly mindless when they're combat-activated, like termites in the mound.'

Sela glanced down at the wasted soldier. 'It's the only way I can see it working. He must have some central control. At the moment these jokers are operating on automatic. Thead must be tied up running external defence – but the moment he gets a whisper that something's wrong down here, he'll go overt and we'll have the whole lot down on us.'

'So we do this fast,' Dredd said. 'Hit his control centre before he has time to react. Where?'

Sela thought about it. 'I don't have anything hard,' she said at last. 'I can only work with where I went and what I saw when I was under – and these sad drokks never let the women see much more than a kitchen and a bed. I remember one thing, though, from one time. I don't really want to talk about it much. Alcoves in what he calls his Inner Sanctum, curtained off. If it's anywhere, it'll be there.'

Brit-Cit

The slugs impacted in a tight grouping over sternum and abdomen. Armitage went down with a small spray of blood. He juddered and gurgled and then was still.

Silence, save for the hammer of the walls, the faint hum of the charger to one side. Cautiously, gun at the ready, the dark figure left his cover and worked his way through the junk of the studio.

The Detective Judge lay sprawled and bleeding,

one arm crushed under him. The dark figure stood over him and regarded him for a moment. 'Scratch one problem.'

'You're so right,' said Armitage, and shot him.

In transition

caught and caught *and head over heels with my heart in my* mouth *bogeymen and juju lights behind their ragged eyes and fall it hurts to* breathe *and there's blood on the walls sick slick mucus on the walls and*
                    something
                    is happening to my
                                        plunging
through a cavern of red and slimy membrane, bulbous tubes and protruding cilia-like formations. Clusters of lights flashed with the light of burning magnesium and, through dark openings, she caught glimpses of white, flat-projected, hideously distorted faces. Her skin loosened and distended, gelid flesh slopped and streamed in her wake and. . .

(*skin and muscle sloughing and reforming something bright and metametallic something bright and strong and something below and oh my oh my grud it's coming big and fast and oh my grud it's as big as the –*)

She hit the soft meat floor of the cavern head-first. There was no actual pain, merely the sensation of a sudden, cushioned halt. Dazed, disorientated, Karyn hauled herself onto her knees.

Clawed human hands and forearms proliferated, sprouting from the fleshy ground like flowers: the flesh had completely rotted to white bone on the forearms themselves, the handbones shrouded in

111

veins and wispy tangles that might have been neurons.

The wet floor glistened. The hands began to move.

The hands scrabbled for her, clutching, clicking, grasping her with a jerking, cloying intimacy and something slid into her head like soft razors, hot and clotted in her *head*.

And she screamed.

And big light came out of her, a reflex-sting of white-hot plasma. The clutching hands went to pieces.

For a while, Karyn lay back in a cooling, solidifying pool of grease and charred bone, gazing up at the red, wet cavern, the lights shining from the walls. After a while she realised that she was holding her hands in front of her face, staring at them dumbly.

They were mirror-bright, like polished chrome. Her whole body was the same.

She became aware of cool, fresh air on her face.

The explosion of plasma had ripped a hole in the wall of the cavern. Bright forms shifted beyond it.

Feet slipping on slick, wet membrane, Karyn headed for the rip.

Chakra Puja, MC1

They went up through the Chakra Puja, Dredd even with his stiff leg keeping up with the Shok-Tac troops if not surpassing them. The rotting bodies choked the corridors and stairwells – it had, after all, been simpler to condition the Faithful to ignore them utterly.

Now, as she followed the uniformed forces, Sela Kane began to feel the cumulative effect – years of

112

deep cover, she realised, could not leave one unchanged. Memories and identity had been locked off and new ones grafted on, a whole secondary personality had been constructed, mapped onto an unused section of her brain and conditioned to self-destruct given the correct set of circumstances, and with it the conditioning that had twisted an already basic personality . . . but some things go deeper.

She knew that, irrevocably, she was not the woman who had coldly submitted to Justice Department deep-cover processes.

Hatred boiled inside her for the brutalising life she had led, the physical reminders like a ridged lip from where she had been backhanded once, a scar on her arm; the crawling memory of abuses for which the identity that had experienced them had been artificial but the pain and emotions were real.

She had been assigned to get close to a particularly vicious bogtown gang and their leader, Raan. With clear memory now, she remembered how they had ranged Sector 17, how they had joined the ranks of the Faithful: the men as the Soldiers of the Light, acting as enforcers and assassins before Thead's brainwashing processes became more blatant. She remembered how Raan had needed only minimal conditioning to maintain his absolute loyalty. He was, after all, doing what he loved best.

She remembered all the things he had done to her, all the things he had made her do. She was going to kill him, if she could.

And there was something else. Something so vital that it was a part of herself. Something she was forgetting . . .

'What the drokk do you think you're doing, Kane?' Dredd said.

Sela realised that she had lagged behind slightly. She broke into a run and caught the group up. 'Sorry. I was miles away.'

'Don't do it again or we leave you to fend for yourself.'

The stairwell opened up into a large and expensive rec-centre: the original inhabitants of Chakra Puja Block held that while the mortification of the flesh and the exaltation of the spirit was all very well, there was no need to be fanatic about it. Pristine and highly polished weight-lifting and sporting equipment was made slightly less so by the shot bodies hanging off it.

Cautiously the squad headed for one of the doorways set radially around the chamber. They were on Level 16 now, where the Unbelievers had been kept, the corridors piled with the still-steaming bodies of those dragged from their makeshift prisons and torn to pieces.

One or two things that might once have been human groaned, one or two limbs flopped weakly. There was no other movement.

'Oh, Jovus,' Sela said weakly. 'He's done them all.'

'So now we take him out,' said Dredd. 'Tell me about it.'

'Okay.' Sela reeled off points automatically. 'You can hit the Level 17 central chapel from the south, west or north. The east access leads into Thead's inner sanctum and I don't know where it goes from there. If he's simply taken the cult back there, you have maybe five hundred warm bodies. You can

114

discount most of them unless he triggers another mob-frenzy, and you'll sort of notice that anyway.

'Soldiers of the Light you already know about, and if there are any in there it's just a case of doing them before they do you. The people you really have to watch out for, though, are the Principalities. Hessian robes, but more elaborate ones than the rest of the cult. Flaming brands embroidered on their chests. The Principalities are Thead's lieutenants and they're relatively sophisticated and cunning. You got me?'

'Okay.' Dredd worked the autoload and checked the microcircuitry of his Lawgiver. The Shok-Tak troops loaded fresh clips into their assault guns.

'But listen, Dredd,' said Sela. 'Once the shooting starts, the free-ranging soldiers are going to land on us with both feet. We'll be boxed in there, in the chapel. They could cut us to pieces.'

'Don't worry about it,' Dredd said. 'Siege Command's been tracking us and they're ready with diversionary tactics. That should give these Soldiers of the Light more than enough to worry about.'

As if on cue, there came the sound of muffled detonations as the forces outside launched a new assault.

Brit-Cit

The car following them, Treasure explained, was a stalker: little more than a body shell, an engine and a guidance system. There were any number of them in the city, cruising on automatic, sonar- and transponder-shielded, stopping only to recharge.

The remaining space was packed with heavy-duty

sensors and hi-ex. A stalker had one simple function: it was given a target and it latched onto it. The moment the target's power gave out, or the moment anything bigger than a rat tried to leave it, the hi-ex detonated.

Theoretically, of course, one could prolong the time before detonation by simply keeping on the move. The problem with this was that this would require some perpetually self-recharging power source – and the combined incomes of a non-back-hander-taking Judge and an up-and-coming installation artist barely stretched to a couple of second-hand power cells only good for a couple of days on one charge, and last charged up a couple of days ago.

Terry had swung them back up onto the orbital and switched to auto-cruise: actual speed was neither here nor there. The initial shock of Dispatch cutting them loose had devolved into a sort of calm and sad acceptance. Treasure scanned the interway intently, looking for some anomaly, some miraculous means of escape – but this was automatic; she knew that there was no hope of rescue.

An LED was blipping on the dash. 'We're on back-up,' Treasure said. 'Twenty minutes, half an hour tops.'

And it was at this point that the mobile phone racked by the two-way began to bleep.

'Steel?' the voice of Detective Judge Armitage said. 'Where are you? What's happening?'

Parareality

A vast, multidimensional structure dopplering to infinity through a depri-sensory gulf; an interlocking network of abstract structures and, within each, an infinity of images: fish with lanterns on stilts; dead tables, catslit-eyed; a telephone scarred by a barbed-wire fence; eating people in the back seat; insurgents underwater . . .

A weak-chinned doctor advancing on a rubber doll clutching a gas-mask, a snipping windshield a horse under a wall and she losing co she cocococo losing co she –

It was impossible and dislocated and insane; Karyn felt whole areas of her mind flowering under its light. It was some time before she noticed that she had drifted from the lip of the hole – which had promptly sealed itself shut behind her.

Disorientated, she skimmed back towards what she hoped was her starting point.

And then she realised that she was flying.

For a while she didn't feel up to anything more than soaring and whooping through the abstract web, lost in the simple joy of unrestrained kinesthesia.

Eventually she got a grip on herself, reminded herself that she was supposed to be here to do a job.

On the extreme edge of her perceptions, she saw small specks moving, lazily sculling through the gulf. A couple of them appeared to have noticed her, were heading vaguely in her direction.

Karin decided to meet them. She rotated herself laterally through a couple of dimensions and accelerated forward.

After a while, she saw that the specks were part of a larger, farther swarm. A million? A billion? Far too many to count.

Closer now, and the nearest, the outriders of the swarm resolved themselves into dark, obloid pellets.

Closer now again. Details became distinct.

And Karyn began to scream. The same word over and over and over again.

Brit-Cit

After checking the studio for other possible assailants, moving slightly clumsily due to the body-armour under his trenchcoat, Armitage located a phone on a work bench and slotted in a call-protection wafer.

He had been on his way out of the apartment, when 'Taea had chimed up, mentioning – on the vague off-chance that he might be interested – that Treasure's call might be the result of an extremely sophisticated synthesizer, but it was definitely synthetic. And who exactly do you think you're telling to piss off?

Armitage's veins felt raw and desiccated from the Anti-Tox he had shot into himself. The left side of his face was bleeding from a deep gouge caused by shrapnel from the fragmenting slugs.

Still, he reflected, it could have been worse. The guy might have gone for the head – highly unlikely, since such a relatively small and mobile target was far more difficult to hit than the main mass of the body, but he might have found himself up against some flash git.

He had checked his two-way and found transmissions jammed – and knew enough to realise what that meant. If Steel was still alive, the only way she could be contacted at this point was by her personal phone.

The phone bleeped a couple of times and was picked up.

'Steel,' Armitage said. 'Where are you? What the drokk's going on?'

A small intake of breath on the other end.

'Steel?'

Then the voice of Steel began to speak calmly, detailing her situation briefly and without fuss: 'I'm in the car. Terry's with me. Stalker on our tail. Maybe twenty minutes of power left. Do you need a repeat?'

'Jovus . . .' Armitage said. 'You've been cut loose, too?'

'Yes.'

'Okay.' Armitage thought about it for a moment. 'Listen, I'll make some calls, try to set something up. You give me your exact location and best-guess where you're heading. And then all you can do is wait.'

Parareality

The thing was huge. If it had been applicable to human sensory terms it would have been hundreds of miles across. Flesh and wood and clockwork, tentacles flickering against the fabric of the abstract web and wounding it, damaging it on some fundamental and inexpressible level.

And it was crooning.

The howling madness of it threatened to drown

119

Karyn's mind. *How can it live*, she thought frantically. *How can something like that* live?

And all the time her mouth worked and screamed.

She never saw it until it was way, way too late. A barbed and chitinous hook, a fleshy, slimy cord training behind it, took her in the mouth.

It burst through the nape of her neck. The barbs extended and bit into her flesh with a sickening *clunch*!

The pain was immense. It was a pain which on the physical plane would be mercifully ended by instant death.

But she didn't die.

The thing hauled her in like a fish on a line.

Engulfed her.

Chakra Puja, MC1

The block was shifting, warping, its geodesic skeleton compensating for the force of the explosions outside.

Dredd sent the Shok-Tac troops through the south door of the chapel in an alternate-spread pattern, their streamlined impulses switched to pattern recognition and reaction: see a Soldier of the Light, kill a Soldier of the Light.

Such a confrontation, with the Soldiers of the Light similarly conditioned, was entirely automatic, the physical equivalent of running a sorting program through a transputer – and operated upon a barely higher level of speed. Gunfire blazed without a break for four seconds before becoming sporadic.

Dredd went through the door fast, Sela behind him. They hit the floor and rolled in opposite directions, Dredd finding cover behind the fallen armoured body of a Shok-Tac.

He saw that maybe thirty soldiers had been in the chamber – all of them now down. Retaliatory fire had taken out most of his own troops, but there were two left – one missing her left arm from the elbow, automatically sealed and cauterised by her suit, one relatively intact. They had switched to their more complex responses now, and had turned their attention to the figures Sela Kane had described as the Principalities, and for which Dredd had sanctioned summary execution.

Thead's lieutenants, it appeared, had not been armed with anything more than electro-rods. A number of them had scored assault rifles from dead Soldiers of the Light. Two of these were holed up behind a bloodstained dais beneath a stained-glass window on the east wall. A curtained archway was set into the wall by the window: Thead's inner sanctum.

Dredd brought up his Lawgiver. 'Heat-seeker,' he snapped.

The gun's microsystems switched in the appropriate ammunition chamber. Dredd pulled the trigger twice. The heat-seeking shells shot in curving trajectories, circumnavigating the dais on either side and hit the two men, simultaneously throwing them back in a couple of sprays of blood.

Dredd went through the chapel as the battle raged around him, dodging the occasional bullet from one of the Faithful who still had a gun.

Around him, the lower orders of the cult, the rank-and-file and the women and children, sat vacant and dazed and uninterested, moving only vaguely

121

and ineffectually if they moved at all. The fact that some of them had been hit by gunfire, had been killed or horrifically wounded, did not seem to trouble them at all.

Dredd reached the dais and confirmed his two kills – a heat-seeker, being packed with sensors and guidance systems rather than explosives or shrapnel, tended to be problematic. One of his targets was dead, an entrance-wound in his throat, a gaping hole in the back of his head. The other had been hit in the shoulder and was out of it with shock. Dredd left him to it.

He turned his attention to the archway.

And then he paused. There was nothing concrete, nothing he could put his finger on, but this seemed too obvious. Too easy.

He raised his Lawgiver and aimed it at the curtain, then tracked it to the stained glass window – took it out with a standard round and dived through the biofluorescent panelling and shattered glass.

Brit-Cit

The LED continued to flash red as the back-up cells leeched dry. Treasure hit the dash with the heel of her hand in the vague, emotional and irrational hope that the display would switch to green. It went dead altogether.

'Whoops,' Treasure said. 'Y'know, this is probably the point where you say there's something you really have to tell me,' she said to Terry.

Terry shrugged and smiled slightly. 'Most of my acts of appalling depravity tend to have involved you, anyway. Besides, once we get out of this in one piece I'd never hear the end of it.'

'I don't want to rain on your parade, Terry, but getting out of this in one piece isn't much of an option.'

'Of course it is. I have absolute faith in you.' Terry smiled again. 'So you're never going to hear the gory details of that diesel in Bell. Nary a word of electrodes and custard and Wellington boots shall pass my lips.'

Treasure laid her cheek against her spouse's arm. 'Did I ever tell you that I could quite like you, if there's nothing better going?'

'With alarming frequency,' said Terry.

The phone bleeped.

'Steel?' Armitage said. 'How you doing?'

'Not so hot,' said Treasure.

'Yeah, well I think I've got a solution.'

Treasure's heart leapt.

'You should be hitting the Ramp 214 turn-off any minute now, right?' said Armitage.

'Um . . . I think we just passed it,' said Terry.

Treasure's heart sank again.

'Oh stomm . . . no, no, hang about.' A brief pause. 'You can do it from 215, too. It's doable. Listen, Steel, we've got one shot at this so you take the turn-off and then you follow my directions exactly, you got it?'

'I got it,' Treasure said. From the driving seat, Terry nodded.

'And just so you know, Steel, I still haven't forgotten about that pint you owe me.'

'Up yours, you old git,' said Treasure.

123

Parareality

Running through black and twisted trees, briar thorns slicing skin from her face and tiny animal bones crunching underfoot.

She couldn't breathe: *crackle-crust in her throat like the dried discharge from an infected cut, spongy flecks between her teeth. They never stop. They* never *stop. Torchlight behind her and in the chill air the tang of distant burning pitch. Her blood, they want her blood and they're coming for her on her heels . . .*

A faint and breathy chuckle behind her. She swung out blindly, nails tearing through damp, soft flesh, sickeningly warm. Something screamed.

And now the lights were ahead of her.

Something squirmed under her bruised and bloody feet. She pitched forward with a cry, striking the side of her head against a gnarled tree bole. She moaned, hauled herself up and back on her feet by the brass knob, leant heavily, panting, by the door sunk into the tree. The lights were closer and the gibbering voices louder now and they . . .

The door?

Crawled into a small, square wooden cupboard. Hugged her knees until she felt her spine crack. Shafts of cold white light swung across her, one after another, after another. The voices chittered and giggled together, high-pitched and very, very sly:

'. . . a spoon and sharpen it and slide it inside. I want to see what's inside *I want . . .'*

'. . . my certain fingers eating worms. The seventh lock. The seventh single lock and . . .'

124

(The hook burst into her mouth and then there was a *claw*.

Wet black rubber-flesh opened to enfold her. A ribbed bone needle as thick as a forearm stabbed towards her and then she was –)

Turn the world.

Chakra Puja, MC1

Sela hit the floor of the chapel and rolled, kicking out of the way a hessian-clad body decapitated by rapid fire. A figure loomed over her, bald, pale and corpulent in the robes of a Principality, bringing down a sparking shock-rod like a club. Sela brought up her assault rifle one-handed and he danced back with his stomach exploding.

Off to one side, Dredd was firing on a couple of men behind the dais. The surviving Shok-Tacs were picking off the scattered Principalities more or less at random. Sela hauled herself into a semi-crouch and scanned her surroundings.

She looked at the vapid, semi-comatose Faithful with clear eyes for the first time, saw the wasted malnutrition of them, the sores that pocked their skin, the living corruption, the marks of old wounds.

The Faithful had lived in filth and squalor and the rotting dead they had killed, and they had simply never noticed. How could she have lived like this? Even under deep cover, some fundamental part of her must have *known*. How could she have subjected herself and her child to . . .?

Kelli!

Since she had surfaced from deep cover, she had

125

somehow blanked out any and every thought of her child – and now she realised that though she would have liked to think it was a result of Justice Department conditioning, she had done it to *herself*.

The awful weight of what she had done came crashing down. She had done what she had done through conscious choice – had accepted the negation of herself voluntarily. And then she had allowed an innocent child who had no choice in the matter to suffer years of systematic abuse. Her own child.

Her stomach constricted, spasmed. She choked.

And the shockrod charge arced through her with a crack.

A foot kicked her over. She lay on her back, unable to do anything but shake. Around her, the confusion and struggle of the battle.

A hazy figure stood over her, smiling down at her, idly playing with his shockrod and all but insensate to the chaos around him.

'I loved you,' Raan said. 'I really did. I loved you and you betrayed me.'

Brit-Cit

Terry steered the car into an industrial site that must have been derelict since the Civil War. Vegetation sprouted from the cracks between concrete paving, some of which had long-since crumbled. Later, when she had time to replay the events etched onto her memory, Treasure realised that there was something out of place here: damage to the weeds caused by vehicles running over them recently had been almost perfectly concealed.

Since they took the exit ramp, Armitage had directed them through a maze of sidestreets rather suspiciously empty of traffic. The matt-black car followed, slowing when they slowed, accelerating when they accelerated, slowly creeping up on them until there were a few metres between them, as though sensing that its target was near to exhaustion. And with the read-outs on the fritz, Treasure knew, there would be no warning.

'Now listen,' the voice of Armitage said. 'You see a warehouse with a "Plant Hire" sign over it? There should be a set of doors in the side. They should be open.'

'We see it,' said Treasure.

'Slow down and go through them. Keep driving dead slow. At some point you're going to see a signal of some sort, and then I want you to give it all you've got, okay.'

'I got it,' Terry said. The car slowed to a crawl. The stalker followed.

Through the doors, in the dim light, Treasure could just make out a path leading through a number of flat planes running off at an angle on either side. Blast shields. Between them, a number of large, circular copper half-rings.

'As I live and breathe,' Treasure said cheerfully. 'Stasis coils.'

They crawled through the blast shields, the stalker following behind.

And then, an accelerating, throbbing whine behind them. In the rear-view mirror the coils began to glow. Slowly the distance between them and the stalker began to increase.

Red flarelight burst in front of them. Terry hit the accelerator.

And the power gave out.

And behind them the stalker detonated.

Chakra Puja, MC1

Pale ambient light spilled, flickering, through the remains of the window. Biofluorescent shards lay scattered and bright.

Dredd came through into a rough-walled space maybe three metres in depth and as wide as the chapel's entire wall.

To his right, on the periphery, the archway that led from the chapel – and standing in wait was the bulky form of a Soldier of the Light. Dredd was bringing his Lawgiver round before he hit the floor and . . . and then he paused.

The soldier stood, slightly slumped, absolutely still.

Cautiously, gun switched to armour-piercing and at the ready, he prowled towards the soldier and examined him. Immobile and unbreathing, his face flushed with the deceptively healthy glow of one who has died barely a minute before.

Outside, the fighting was dying down.

In the wall opposite the archway was a second opening, something glowing warm and redly from within, like firelight. Dredd went through it doing all the right stuff.

A spacious living chamber, comfortable without being ostentatious, warm light playing on the walls. Most of the floorspace was taken up by sculpted padding and cushions.

In an alcove in the far wall, banks of communications and control equipment. A bio-feed headset hung over the back of a padded chair. There were no items of a religious nature of any kind.

Absolom Leviticus Thead sat calmly upon a couple of cushions, dressed in a neat, dark suit, hands clasped rather primly around his knees.

His eyes were clear and kind and gentle.

'I knew you'd come,' he said quietly. 'It was just a matter of time. I waited for you.'

Parareality

Rap, rap, rapping of knuckles on wood. Knuckles rap-rapping on wrapping wood.

'I know you're in there, you know. Won't you come out?'

A pleasant voice, friendly and full of secrets. It was a trick. She stayed very small and still and held her breath.

'I'm still here,' the voice said. 'And *you're* still there. Don't you remember me? I'm Jackie Pelt. I'm the toyman. Don't you remember?'

'I remember you,' she said. 'I made you. I own you. You're mine.'

'But of *course* I'm yours.' The voice laughed happily. 'You're the goddess, you're the creator-mother. You made me out of spit and string. So how can I hurt you?'

'Listen.' The voice became conspiratorial. 'The change monster isn't the only one who can make things happen. I can make them happen, too. I can make things *right*.

'Won't you come out?'

129

Karyn thought about this. 'Could you open the door yourself if you wanted to?' she asked suspiciously.

A chuckle. 'I could open it. Just like *that*. But it's *your* door. It's your choice. Won't you come out?'

The lock turned with a soft satisfying click. The door sprung open and she tumbled out of the box.

Into:

Her bedroom. It had all been a dream. Everything was all right.

Jackie Pelt was sitting in her cot, playing idly with a red-haired doll, idly bending its arms and legs back and forth: a tall, thin man in pitch black and a battered stovepipe hat. Pale face, stringy black hair and wide, strange eyes. A swirling black and yellow tie around his neck.

He was just as she remembered him.

Jackie Pelt smiled at her warmly, then glanced at the doll. 'Do you like it? It's for you.' He tossed it to her.

She caught the doll automatically and peered at it. She had thought it was made of polymer, but it felt like flesh. Its eyes were closed and it was smiling. It seemed to be about fifteen years old, ten years older than herself.

'Do you like it?' Jackie Pelt snapped his fingers, and suddenly the doll was wearing a dress, polka-dotted and sky blue. 'I told you I can make things happen.'

He snapped his fingers again: a shimmering fairy-tale evening gown of tissue-thin silk. 'I can do anything you want,' Jackie Pelt crooned.

Again: a scarlet riding jacket and jodhpurs. 'I can give you what you *need* . . .'

And again: a leather jacket and a short leather skirt, the words 'BOX BOX BOX' scrawled in shocking pink.

The bedroom lurched. She was thrown off her feet, hit the mirror set into the wardrobe door heavily with her shoulder. It shattered.

The room lurched again. She staggered to her feet, ran for the window and threw the curtains back:

A red and swirling sky. A vast, dry, cracked plain; thunderheads on the horizon, the flare of sheet lightning.

The ropes sweeping down to the hunched creatures as they crawled across the plain and hauled the room behind them.

Movement behind her. She spun round.

The grinning face of Jackie Pelt bobbed before her – and one eye bulged, the face and atrophied body warping away from it, lips curled back from rotten teeth.

And she could hear the twisted, leprous words in his head as they wriggled and squirmed and ate each other with their tiny, sawtoothed mouths: '. . . said I'm not going to hurt you,' he giggled, 'and I *won't* (but) . . . I won't (but) . . . I'm not going to lay a *hand* on you (but oh but oh but oh but *oh*) . . .'

He lunged for her. Swollen fingers jerked and snapped.

His hands never touched her, moulding themselves around her a bare fraction of a millimetre from her flesh.

The mouth opened wider. A tongue unrolled.

'You made me!' Jackie screamed. 'You made us all! (and slit and slit and *slit* you slither hole you eat

131

and slit) And this is our place, and now you're here, we can do what we *like*.'

Wet red mouth loomed towards her until it filled her entire field of vision.

Sector 8 (Chakra Puja), MC1

When Dredd and his squad had hit the sixteenth floor, the forces outside had bombarded the block from all sides – low-power charges intended to keep the defensive forces occupied rather than to cause serious damage. The Justice Department forces inside the block had maintained radio silence and there was no hard data on what was a legitimate target and what was not.

From the command centre, Tek-Judges watched the remote-controlled drones as they spun and swooped on their impellers, strafing the block, falling to pieces under the returning fire.

Abruptly the retaliation stopped.

'Jovus!' a Tek-Judge whose name was Traven exclaimed. 'Will you look at *that*?'

'They're withdrawing?' one of his fellows said.

'No.' Traven tapped at a monitor with a gauntleted finger. 'Look at the read-outs. Look at the *life* signs.'

New Old Bailey, Brit-Cit

In the New Old Bailey, the tranquility of the main entrance hall was suddenly rent asunder by a slightly battered Detective Judge Armitage and a slightly scorched Judge Treasure Steel. As they burst through the doors, they glanced around themselves with some small surprise.

Even for a Saturday night, the place was in chaos. Uniformed Judges dragged struggling, shrieking figures towards the holding pens, occasionally subduing them with the Mega-City-issue daysticks that had caused such a marked increase in accidental deaths since they had been introduced.

Off to one side, Treasure saw an old woman earnestly explaining to her arresting Judge that the young had no respect these days and must be disciplined. Her arms were slathered with dried blood to the elbows. Beyond her she saw a restrained and hysterically struggling figure wearing the ragged remains of a Judge uniform.

'Jovus . . .' she said. 'What's been happening while we've been out having fun? Do you think this is why our two-ways were blocked?'

'Don't you believe it,' Armitage growled. 'Listen, we should be safe here if we make a lot of noise about it. It's too public for anyone to try anything overt – but the moment we go somewhere out of the way, the hammer comes down again. We were lucky, and we might be lucky again, but they only have to be lucky once.'

Treasure nodded. The stasis coils in the ostensibly deserted warehouse had slowed the stalker drone's processes down a little and the blast shields had deflected most of the force, but the car had flipped over, only to be doused with inert foam by a group of ragged men in the feather and leather of a jackgang – although Treasure knew, instantly, that there was no *way* these characters were a jackgang at all.

133

The leader of the group, a tall, cheerfully grinning muscular man with a Cocteau tattoo, had waved an airy hand to silence Treasure and Terry's thanks.

'Tell Armitage that this squares him and us. It's no big deal; we keep these rigs on stand-by for when the competition gets a little boisterous. As for you, though, I want you both to listen carefully now.

'Sometime, maybe next week, maybe next year, maybe even never, you're going to get a call from someone calling himself by the rather unlikely name of Mr Hooty. Yeah, I know, but I don't want there to be any confusion about it. The good Mr Hooty will ask you to do a favour. You will do this favour. You have my word, for what it's worth, that this favour will not involve the destruction of innocent life.'

Treasure opened her mouth to speak, and again the man gestured her into silence.

'I know what you're going to say,' he said. 'This has nothing to do with saving you from a fiery death. What it's about is you walking out of here.'

Treasure had looked into his cheerful eyes and nodded, knowing that this intangible obligation was now sunk into her head like an itch she would never be able to scratch.

They had reached a duty desk. Armitage shoved a couple of auxiliaries out of the way and glowered at the duty Judge.

'You get Warner down here *now*.'

'I'm sorry, sir,' the duty Judge said. 'All Senior Judges are directing operations for this current emergency.' He might have been reading from a script.

'Yeah. I thought the place had gone mad.' Armi-

134

tage reached over the counter and grabbed the startled duty Judge by the lapel.

'Listen, sunshine,' Armitage growled in his face. 'You get me Senior Judge Warner now, in person, or we won't be held responsible for my actions.'

Beside him, without being overtly threatening, Treasure had pulled the gun she had used in the Tight White bust from her jacket and examined it critically. The duty Judge considered his options, and made the call.

Chakra Puja, MC1

'On your feet,' Dredd growled, gesturing slightly with his gun. 'Cross to the wall and spread. One move towards me and you go down.'

'Such suspicion,' Thead smiled slightly, indulgently even. 'I do not shout something like "Eat plasma, motherdrokker!" and try to shoot you, and you don't know how to respond. Do you expect some final trick, some invisible force-field protecting me, some coating of venom that will kill you if you touch me? It must all be a bit of an anti-climax for you.' Thead rose from his cushions, walked to the wall and assumed the position.

Dredd frisked him and cuffed him.

'This is hardly necessary, you know,' Thead said. 'I'll give you no trouble for the simple reason that there is *nothing* you can do to me, fundamentally. Incarcerate or kill me, I am whole and pure in spirit and I am in a state of Holy Grace.'

'Oh yeah,' Dredd said with disgust. 'Really holy.'

Thead shrugged. 'I know what you mean. You think that all this . . .' automatically, he attempted a sweeping gesture before realising he was cuffed, 'you think that this is charlatanism, pure and simple. Lure in the confused and the inadequate and the insane and give them something to worship and hate, fill them with second-hand garbage and compulsive quasi-ritual, and thus achieve some absolute control.

'And you're quite right. But only on one level.

'You see, this is what a religion is, on a level far deeper than mere words or icons. It is not the specifics that are important, but the structure itself. The acolytes must have restrictions – and not necessarily sexual – the more rigid and complicated and self-contradictory the better. The masters must . . . but I see I am boring you. You must forgive me. I tend to get a little over-enthusiastic when I warm to my favourite theme.

'Ah well.' Thead smiled wistfully to himself. 'I must admit that your arrival caused me to, um, accelerate my programme a little, but the terminal phase took place, I believe, remarkably smoothly.'

'What?' Dredd had switched Thead off somewhere around 'second-hand garbage and compulsive quasi-ritual', and had been examining the consoles: hypno-strobe and psycho-active odorizer co-ordinators, subsonic generators, heavy-duty surveillance systems . . . Thead must have known exactly where he and his squad were every minute from the start. '*What*?'

Thead shrugged. 'Any religion is just a system for sending a suitably encoded transmission – a "soul", if you like – to the spiritual plane. Death, in itself, is just the carrier signal – and mass-death increases the volume.

136

'Over the last few hours, my Principalities have administered to the Faithful . . . every man, woman, infant and child – eucharists impregnated with a certain psycho-active toxin, relatively painless and very, very fatal. I do believe they had just about completed the procedure when you burst into the chapel.'

New Old Bailey, Brit-Cit

Warner seemed flustered. 'Armitage. I heard you had a little, ah . . .'

'Right,' said Armitage. 'Odd, you knowing that, seeing how the two-ways were buggered.'

Warner's face fell. 'I . . . I don't know what you – '

'Leave it,' Armitage growled. 'Just so you *do* know, a certain person or persons unknown tried to kill me and Steel tonight – very slick, very neat, and as is probably quite obvious, with a marked lack of success.

'That gave me time to react. Scattered around the city are a number of dormant info-bombs. They've been there for years. I've activated a couple of them – Steel or I die in suspicious circumstances and lots of interesting data gets dumped into the net.

'Now, something like that is not a lot of use unless you actually tell people about it. So I'm telling everyone I can think of. You be sure to pass it around, yeah?'

Chakra Puja, MC1

'Who have you consorted with?' Raan said as he stood over his collapsed and jerking woman as she tried to raise herself, oblivious to the carnage around them. 'With whom have you *lain*? Who has filled your head with these evil, *evil* thoughts?'

He paused for a moment, pleased with the alliterative effect of his monologue, then rather than waiting for a reply, he continued magnanimously. 'I forgive you. You are a whore and a betrayer . . . but I forgive you.' He smiled kindly. 'I will see that this filth is eradicated from you.'

Sela looked up into his mad eyes and idiotic grin, and remembered the post-hypnotic triggers of the drastically simplified society of the Faithful that had made her fear and worship him – and suddenly collapsed into choking, hysterical laughter.

'Oh my Grud, you're a pompous little prick,' she spluttered.

This response, so utterly at odds with his natural impulses let alone his imposed conditioning, staggered Raan. For a moment he stared at her aghast.

And bracing her shoulders against the filthy floor Sela racked her leg back and pile-drove a foot into him with all the precise force that Justice Department combat-training and teak-hard muscle from years of surreptitious and unconsciously performed exercising could muster.

It would, of course, Sela thought, have been far more satisfying to go for the obvious target – but she had had enough. She went for the kill. The heel of her foot bludgeoned into his abdomen under the ribcage, explosively rupturing several internal organs, the force travelling directly to the spine and shattering it with a crackle and pop of vertebrae. The force of the blow knocked Raan up and off his feet to land on top of a dead Shok-Tac in a twisted and unnatural angle.

Watchfully, Sela climbed into a semi-crouch. Her skin still prickled with pins and needles, but her reflexes seemed okay.

The fighting was dying down. One Shok-Tac had the few remaining Principalities pinned down in an alcove containing a defaced icon of Kloi Kloi Seki. The other was under cover, scanning the chapel doors for the possible arrival of enemy reinforcements. There was no sign of Dredd, but the stained-glass window in the east wall was shattered. She had, she remembered, heard a loud crash a while back.

Sela left them to it. She had made her decision – and, having made it, she was surprised about how good she felt.

The Justice Department ran extensive rehab programmes for Wally Squad operatives – who could, after all, work for years on a single case, acquiring any number of emotional attachments on the way. Even without the complications of children, a Wally Squad Judge was always offered the option of an honourable discharge with pension on the completion of a job.

The Justice Department psychs would repair the damage caused to her child in his first traumatic years, and then Sela would take the discharge. They would cut out any sensitive information in her head, of course, but they were welcome to it. She had had enough.

She scanned the lethargic crowd of the rank-and-file Faithful, looking for her child.

Parareality. The Bunker

It peeled her, layer by layer; everything she ever had been was flensed away into the void. Shrieking, screaming, bubbling to white bone.

And then, with no warning, the power surged through her, distending her, chaoplasm channelled through her, twisting into images, personas, whole interlocking universes of identity:

(*A woman with vulpine eyes ranges a landscape of molten glass and sobbing. The face of the child is featureless, perfectly smooth.*

A man with a stunted parasite claws at his face with ragged, broken nails, and screams. His skin is like wax; his nails leave bloodless furrows.

A sculpted, wooden parody of a dog flexes greased rope tendons and drags itself across the yellow grass. A man in a striped blazer and straw boater watches it for a while, then turns his mad eyes up to the sun . . .

Image upon image upon image. The wheels spin too fast. Bloody-fingered deities look into your eyes with inhuman love as they pull your lights steaming from you and eat them. That's all they do. . .)

The stomach in which we find ourselves is too *small*, its alien enzymes unable to cope. The only option that remains is to sick it up.

Hanging in the gulf. Below her the burst and shredded remains of something other, a force other than

140

physical wrenching her at an impossible angle and *pulling*.

Turn the world.

She cohered with shocking abruptness, like crystals forming in a supersaturated solution.

Looming over her, a monstrosity of rotted flesh and tarnished cybernetics. Dead-lights blazed from the eyes inside its ragged cowl.

'Thank Jovus for that,' it said in a rattling, clicking voice that sounded as though it issued from clockwork. 'You were nearly gone for good. You wouldn't believe how long it took me to reconstruct an identity gestalt.

'And will you stop drokking screaming for a minute? It's me, okay? It's Moloch.'

INTERLUDE

Someone Special (A Tale From a Disrupted City)

Michael went through the motions again: ten-second sweeps of the room, catch an eye for five and smile . . . pushing thirty from barely the right end and feeling every minute of it, he was, he reflected, getting too old for this. The darkly handsome face in the mirrored wall behind the bar was looking just a little too seedy, the eyes just a little too hollow. He could remember when this had been fun.

The place was crowded, happy couples and groups in the alcoves and hermetic mini-smoking booths, singles hunting other singles.

Across the bar under a buzzing UV, a slim woman in something blazing white talked animatedly with a low-grade exec in front of the 12-hour cohab contract dispenser, waiting while it ran the blood and DNA samples. Good luck to you matey, Michael thought, recognising her. Lorna something. Into mutual aura-massage and people keeping their hands to themselves.

Michael recalled the riveting evening he had spent with her while she had explained at great length about how it was a beautiful, sharing, *conceptual* thing. Michael had caught a glimpse of her bedroom in passing: pink and frilly and piled high with stuffed and fluffy toys. He couldn't be sure, but he had the horrible feeling that home-made male genitalia had been stitched onto them.

The dating scene in Mega-City One, at least that subsection themed around certain attitudes and activities prevalent in the later twentieth century, was fraught with danger for man, woman or beast given the number of crazies around – but of late the people whom Michael attracted had tended to fall into the category of being crazy and dangerous without actually being any fun. He bought another synthetic and alcohol-free scotch from the chrome and polyprop-pneumatic bar automaton and looked around again – and found himself looking into the hungry and predatory eyes of a tall electric blonde. Oh Jovus, he thought, she's on the loose again. She's going to land on some poor simp with both four-inch spikes . . .

He remembered her appearing in a doorway, a growling thing with matted hair and cyber-implants straining from a leash. 'Take it easy,' she had said. 'Take it *easy*. I brought him home for *you*, my darling. Just for you.' All of this addressed to the slavering creature in tones of happy, indulgent love.

Michael had been inordinately grateful that he had insisted upon panic-snaps rather than knots.

Somebody special, Michael thought. Somebody normal, that's all I want. Somebody, he added as he caught sight of a pale woman drifting calmly through the crowd in a black and diaphanous long-sleeved cloak, who doesn't consider opening a couple of her own veins with a scalpel blade as basic foreplay.

'Excuse me.'

Michael realised that he had been staring glumly into his drink. He turned toward the sudden presence by his side.

A woman in her mid-twenties with ash-blonde, swept-back hair and level, steady, faintly amused eyes. A two-piece black suit worn with simple elegance, slim gold bands encircling her left wrist and throat.

'Listen.' She took in the surroundings with ironic eyes. 'I know this place is pretty retro-hetero and the men are supposed to go talk to the women, but you looked sort of lonely. Do you want to buy me a drink?'

Her name was Susan Delaney. She worked for GenCom ('The biogenic engineering complex with a human face!') in public relations, relaying the responses of the corporate transputer mainframe via a subcutaneous chip behind her right ear. She was not a regular on the retro scene, she told him, but enjoyed it occasionally for the sense of tension.

'I have this ideal man in my head,' she said as she sipped a cocktail with a name that would be hard-pushed to dignify itself as a single entendre. 'I can see him in my head. It's like he's with me all the time.

'I can see him in people. I mean, your eyes, Michael.' She reached up a hand and gently brushed his temple with slim fingers. 'You have wonderful eyes.'

Two hours later, Michael drove his car up the ramp of the Julie Christie hab-block. He still felt good – but there was something slightly forced about this now. For a while now he had felt a sense of growing

145

pressure, like the charge of static that if left unearthed by Mega-City Climate Control would result in a thunderstorm. His thoughts were disrupted. It was becoming increasingly difficult to think coherently.

It had been impossible to see clearly from the interways, but as he drove he had caught snatches of distant activity, faint flashes and concussion, the glimpse of ant-like people spilling from a block. The car's entertainment system was on the fritz, programming drowned out by static.

Julie Christie Block did nothing to dispel his sense of unease; dark and looming and run-down, small upper sections of its outer structure had sheared from the geodesics, never to be replaced. Lights blazed from the intact levels but the block seemed derelict, probably not maintained since the Apocalypse War.

'This is where you live?' he said.

'I know,' Susan said as they walked through mildewed corridors almost entirely unlit by the sporadic, fizzing neon. 'It's pretty awful, but it's only temporary. I'm due for relocation soon, I think.'

'How soon?' There was a stink like an open drain. Some of the doors were missing off their hinges. Yellow Justice Department tape fluttered in their maws.

'Susan?' Michael said, realising that she had fallen slightly back from him. 'Did you hear me? I said – '

A slim hand clamped over his mouth with surprising strength. A warm, soft body pressed itself close to his back, and before Michael had time to react, something cold and sharp stung the side of his neck.

* * *

146

'Michael?'

Formless shapes swum in front of his eyes, grey and black and white and skin-tone.

'Michael?'

The forms cohered. A relieved Susan smiled down at him like a happy child.

'Hello,' she said. 'Are you feeling better now? I thought I'd given you too much of the sedative. I was quite worried . . .'

Michael tried to speak – and with a cold jolt of terror realised that his mouth was filled with something globular and rubbery – secured, the constricting pressures around his cheeks and the nape of his neck told him, by some sort of polymer-sheathed flex.

A small and absolutely neat bed-sitting apartment, bare of ornamentation, furnishings arranged with precision at right-angles to each other. He was flat on his back, tied to a reclining chair by lengths of grey electrical flex presumably a match for the stuff securing the ball gag.

Beneath him, he felt that the upholstery was covered with polyethylene sheeting.

'I only did it so you wouldn't leave, Michael.' Susan was by the bed, absently rooting through a hold-all in which things clattered and clunked. 'You have to believe that. I just didn't think you'd understand. It's your eyes, you see. Your eyes are, ah . . .'

On the bed, something bulky lay covered with a sheet.

Susan pulled a gouge with a curved blade from the hold-all and inspected it critically, set it aside for the moment.

'I made it myself,' she said. 'It was quite difficult. Look.' She pulled back the sheet with happy pride.

A bloated, stitched lump of meat assembled from various bodies. A scar in its abdomen had burst its stitching. Its mouth hung open, filled with a fluid corruption seeping and crusting on its chin and neck.

'Isn't he beautiful?' Susan said. 'I can't make him move and some of him has rotted, but that's okay. I can make that better.

'When he can see me, you see, I can wake him up. I can make him love me when he has eyes.'

SLICE FOUR

Gods in a Box

The Bunker

Karyn looked glumly down at the worn cybernetic manipulators that were her hands. Her vision sparked and flared with grainy static, sensations stripped to the bare digital minimum. It was like being trapped inside a malfunctioning and misfiring VR unit.

They were in a smallish dome-like chamber walled with some dark golden alloy. White, perpetually renewing biolighting was sunk into the ceiling. Around the walls were banks of consoles of an archaic design. Crude designs had been scrawled over various surfaces in black mud.

The chamber also contained a number of couches. On each of these, hooked to control units by jack leads, lay other cybernetic creatures.

The creature currently inhabited by Moloch was fiddling experimentally and ineptly with a console that seemed like a cross between a state-of-the-art transputer and a bakelite radio set.

'I woke up here,' he was saying in his rattling clockwork voice, 'and there were all these funny little geeks gathered around me. Undercity. They took one look at me and started *salaam*ing and carrying on like all get-out. What I think is, this was some sort of advance warning station once. The operators kept on manning it even after the city was covered over, passing it onto their descendants, and the whole thing just got cargo-culted.' He indicated a smartcard lodged in one of the consoles. 'I reckon they went through their ritual and eventually hit on this. That's what activated this whole set-up.

'I chased them out and checked over this stuff – and eventually I hit this playback routine. It spelled the whole thing out in simple words – I think whoever set this up was thinking in terms of centuries.

'It seems that this place is just one huge system to control and directly access into the higher levels of reality – call it *para*reality. It helps you structure and order it, build an identity gestalt that can survive. Grud alone knows how it works – this stuff's a hundred years old at the very least. I have the ghastly feeling that if you took the covers off you'd find radio valves.'

'That's how you saved me from the . . .?' Karyn trailed off. The feel of the clacking mechanics in her artificial throat was horrendous. She had read that in the days when, say, something like gender reassignment was irreversible, a subject who was not a true transsexual would go insane through the absolute and fundamental shock of suddenly having a body that wasn't theirs. This, she thought, was akin to that – and the body she was currently inhabiting wasn't even *animal*.

'Yeah,' Moloch said absently. 'I was just messing

about really, trying to familiarise myself with the operating system – and then everything went ape.

'It seems that you broke out into paraspace and managed to generate a construct on your own – nice job, by the way. I gather that I was basically an invisible squiggle. Problem was, it took a *lot* of energy to do something like that, and you got noticed.

'When I finally located you, you were in pieces, ripped apart by latent phobic images. I pulled you back and the system took me step-by-step through integrating you and then I decanted you. I'm not sure if I . . . hang on.'

Moloch studied a glowing lozenge read-out and tapped a couple of keys. Karyn instantly felt a lot better. *Touché*, she thought, remembering the Think Tank.

'You can unplug yourself now,' Moloch said.

Karyn did so.

'The . . . thing that attacked me?' she said, stretching slightly fuzzy-feeling but relatively natural fungus and steel legs. 'What was it?'

'Ah,' said Moloch. 'Now, I think that's why we're here. Y'see the paraspace is infested, infected by constructs so alien, so *other* than life as we know it that terms like good or evil don't come into it. They're simply inimical – like a medusa or a basilisk. Their aspect turns you to stone, their touch is death.

'I've read through some of the files on this thing.' He indicated the console with a claw. 'Sometimes it calls itself the Medusa Programme, sometimes it calls itself Section Eight. I get the feeling that it lives some private life of its own. I think there's a lot it isn't telling me – but it's told me this much.

'Its primary function is to protect this reality, our basic reality, from these things. There are certain points where the whole meta-fabric of space-time is weaker than others, where things can get seriously disrupted and where these things can break through. Grud alone knows what would happen if they ever do, but I'd imagine the total annihilation of the physical universe for starters, and then work up.

'And that, I think, is what's happening now.'

Surface Trauma

In Sector 47, in the communal washrooms of the Raoul Hausmann hab-block, Arno Guarechi is scrubbing and scrubbing and scrubbing himself. He is filthy. Filthy. He must scrub himself clean.

Already he has exhausted the possibilities of a wire brush. Now he is using caustic soda which he applies directly with his hands. His skin falls from him in seething flaps. His generative organs and most of his stomach have long since been eaten away.

Sector 8 (Chakra Puja), MC1

Aside from the two surviving Shock-Tacs, the only living things to come out of the Chakra Puja were Judges Joe Dredd and Sela Kane, and Absolom Leviticus Thead. When Dredd had hauled the cuffed Thead from his inner sanctum, he had found Kane desperately trying to resuscitate a malnourished child.

When Kane had seen Thead, she had lunged for him with such a frenzied viciousness that Dredd was forced to club her aside and inject her with a sedative.

A transport was hovering by a shattered Level 17 window. Dredd booted Thead across the gap into the hatch and hauled the supine Sela after him.

As the transport descended, Dredd switched in his link with Control. 'Absolom Leviticus Thead. Wilful murder, approximately sixteen thousand counts, subject to body-count. Various other offences pending the half-hour I'm going to need to tot them up. Maximum time-stretch.'

A 'maximum time-stretch' was the ultimate sentence used for a serious perpetrator who somehow escaped being simply blown away during his arrest. Said perpetrator was sealed into a solid-state stasis field, the minimal power for which was supplied by the conversion of matter atom by atom. In theory at least, so long as there was one speck of matter left in the universe, said perpetrator would be preserved. This was as near to immortality as possible, and – and this was the really nasty bit – due to the specific microstructure of the field the perp would be aware of every single second of it.

'*Sorry, Dredd,*' Control said. '*You're in Sector 8, remember? This is a Brit-Cit citizen arrested under InterDep Law. Actual sentencing exceeds your jurisdiction.*'

'What?' Dredd snapped.

'*New Old Bailey informs us that there are several warrants outstanding on Thead. Authorised personnel will extradite him to Brit-Cit for sentencing as soon as possible.*'

'You have got to be drokkin' me, Control!'

'No joke, Dredd. Let it go. We don't need an international incident on our hands.'

Dredd smacked the side of the transport with a fist. He didn't exactly dent the armour-plate, but then again he didn't exactly bruise his fist either.

'Okay Control,' he said coldly. 'Have it your way – but I am not having him held in the Hinterland lockup. He'd probably overpower them with a couple of verses of "Jesus Wants Me for a Sunbeam". I want him held in Halls of Justice Max.'

A brief pause. Then: 'You got it, Dredd.'

The transport grounded with a hiss of hydraulics. Dredd dropped from the hatch and winced as he landed on his injured leg.

'Request some downtime, Control,' he said. 'Medregen.'

'Uh . . . is this priority, Dredd?'

Dredd considered this, clinically evaluating his performance. 'No priority. I can keep going for as long as you need, maybe eighty per cent efficiency.'

'That's good enough. Things have been happening while you've been incommunicado. Psi Division's down. Fifteen per cent of the force are incapacitated. We got whole sectors going crazy . . .'

'Jovus!'

'Yeah, well, apparently he's the only one of those guys who hasn't turned up somewhere yet. We're pulling you out of Sector 8. Get yourself over to Sector 17. City Bottom. Place called the Trenches. Something's going down there and it sounds like it's right up your street.'

154

In Transit (Brit-Cit/MC1)

On the last BMC commercial stratoliner that would run out of Brit-Cit for the foreseeable future, Armitage sat in an aisle seat, strapped in, surlily nursing a polyprop litre bottle of scotch he had terrorised out of an attendant. He did not *care*, he had told the attendant while in the next seat Treasure Steel put a hand over her eyes, if due to circumstances beyond BMC's collective control they were suffering from extreme turbulence. He was going to the most Grud-forsaken city-state on planet Earth, where they were so squeaky-clean substance-wise that they got a buzz off snorting *sucrose*, for drokk's sake, and this would probably be the last chance he (Armitage) would ever have to have a real drink.

The attendant, who had been extensively trained to deal with all manner of difficulties up to and including being the first volunteer to be eaten on the life-raft, had finally cracked when Armitage had threatened to use his Justice Department systems-override smartcard to reroute the flight via the Totalitarian Hegemony of Bangkok, had brought him the bottle and had subsequently spent the rest of the flight hiding in the starboard aft storage locker.

Armitage took a pull on the bottle and handed it to Treasure. 'Sodding typical, isn't it? Some bugger must have thought fast on his feet.' He glared around the cabin at the rows of frightened people. The stratoliner lurched and one or two of said frightened people squealed.

The plainclothes Judge nodded, swallowed and passed the bottle back. 'Shouldn't those bright people of yours be able to cover something like this?'

'No chance.' Armitage snorted. 'This is in the line of duty, right? Some damn psycho needs extraditing back to Brit-Cit, and we're just the guys to do it. The small fact that the world in general and Mega-City One in particular is going whacko round our ears just happens to be one of them there strange coincidences.' He took another belt and passed the bottle.

'So how do we play it?' Treasure said around the neck of the bottle.

'Same as ever. We play it by ear.' Armitage took the bottle again. 'The way things are going, either we're all going to die or we're not. Either way, there's nothing we can do about it – so we just keep our heads down. Remember we're in another country; they do things differently over there.'

Surface Trauma

In the Harvey Malco conapts of Sector 33, rooms come alive and eat their occupants. Mirrors pulse and flex and extend glassy pseudopods to plunge into the eyes of all who look upon them. Escalators dissolve into gaping slit-like maws with churning metallic teeth.

The Trenches, MC1

The killer had been busy. The needles in his flesh, it seemed, were acting as antennae for some miraculous energy, invigorating him and strengthening him

– he seemed stronger even than he had been in his youth.

He did not know where he was. When the secret of travelling through time had been revealed to him by the still, small voice in his soul, he had resolved to travel forward to the year of Our Lord twenty-one hundred and sixteen when, the voice told him, Judgement Day would have occurred and the world would have been transformed into a veritable Heaven on Earth.

This festering garbage pit in the looming caverns of rockcrete had been utterly unexpected. For a moment he had thought, madly, that indeed the Last Trump had sounded and he had found his way into the very maw of Hell. But after wandering for a while and viewing its inhabitants, this Hell had become dismally mundane. He was still in the world of men, and it had simply degenerated even further than he could have imagined.

Well. He would have to do something about this.

Now he wore the bloody rags he had taken from the first of his kills here. They were of a material like calico, but the fibres themselves were perfectly smooth and almost impossible to break. The remains of the words were stitched into the cloth, the most legible of which were USE and RETROGEN, though neither seemed particularly pertinent.

He put the final touches to his most recent demonstration. He had found a rusty nail amongst the garbage and used a small, heavy slab of brick-like material as an impromptu hammer, driving the nail into the boy's forehead and affixing the makeshift sign. The sign said:

157

'But the Lord was not in the wind: and after the wind an earthquake: but the Lord was not in the earthquake; and after the earthquake a fire: but the Lord was not in the fire: and after the fire a still, small voice.'

A timid movement in the wreckage. Like a snake, the killer darted for the warped and partially crushed canopy of a flier that had lodged against some rusting oil drums, and with an inhuman strength and a squeal of metal ripped it aside.

Cowering behind this makeshift cover were four children: three boys and a girl. Spiral whorls on their cheeks. The larger of the children, the leader, snarled at him, poked defensively at him with the spear-tipped pole in his unwithered hand.

Children. Lovely children.

The killer smiled.

The Bunker

For hours they examined the consoles and equipment, trying out possible routines. The archaic readouts flashed abstract and meaningless symbols – and Karyn learnt that when Moloch had spoken of the system 'telling' him things, that this was the literal truth. It seemed to communicate psychically: they would simply know things in their minds.

They learnt how the system would channel the (unspecified) power to them and pilot them through the hierarchies of the paraspace, how it would excise them from it automatically in case of mortal danger.

It was becoming incredibly insistent that said

158

techniques be put into practice: a thrumming pressure in their minds that would not go away.

'We can't put it off forever,' Karyn said.

'Yeah.' Moloch gazed out through the viewing port of the hatch set into the bunker wall, watching the pale and timid forms of the cargo-cultist stand-by operators as they crept through the torchlit darkness beyond, leaving little offerings. 'Okay.'

They hauled their cybernetic bodies onto the couches and jacked themselves into the control pads: a bank of rocker-switches and a trigger switch.

In unison they slapped down the rockers and pulled the triggers.

Turn the world. They went out.

In Transit (MC1)

Central 1 stratoport, the nearest port to the Halls of Justice, was shut down. Apparently the air-traffic control system had suffered some form of major nervous breakdown and was blocking all ground-to-air communications with a spontaneously generated song, which went like this:

> *What is this that I hear?*
> *Upstairs in the attic,*
> *There is an elephant*
> *Riding around on a bicycle*
> *There is an elephant*
> *So* chic *and elegant*
> *With one trunk here*
> *And one tail there.*

It is to be noted that on the BMC flight from Brit-Cit, two drunks, one a middle-aged man, the other a young woman, sang along with it – and continued to do so even when they were out of transmission range, until a number of slightly irate fellow passengers threatened to take away their bottle.

The stratoliner diverted to West 2, more than fifty kilometres from their destination. Armitage and Steel waited until the other passengers had disembarked, then staggered down the exit ramp and stood before the line demarking the point where InterDep Law ended and Mega-City Law began, finishing off the dregs in their bottle before Armitage threw it negligently over his shoulder. It went clunk.

With a cheery salute to the growling Judges on customs-duty, Armitage and Steel simultaneously pulled DeTox hypos from their pockets and injected themselves. Instantly sober, they stepped over the line.

The Justice Department sensors found a number of minute but detectable mutations, the result of genetic drift in a city slightly freer and easier than Mega-City One. The alarm systems went into fits. The Judges brought up their guns.

'Hit the floor, muties,' one of them snarled.

'Who's he calling a mutant?' Treasure said indignantly.

Armitage shrugged. 'I knew our fiendish ruse was doomed to failure. I bet it was our three extra heads that gave it away. We're *Judges*, all right,' he called to the advancing guards. 'I'm going for my ID, okay?'

This took the Mega-City Judges back somewhat. 'Do it slow,' one of them said.

Armitage slowly stuck his fingers into a lapel pocket and withdrew his warrant card.

Their ID checked out. Grudgingly, the Judges tagged them with subcutaneous smartchips that would enable them to pass through the mutation-detectors that proliferated in the city, and let them through.

'Jovus!' Armitage gazed upon the confusion of the stratoport. 'Either this disruption thing took a screaming left into madness, or everything they say about the mega-cities is true.'

Hold-alls slung over their shoulders, they worked their way through the crowd, Armitage inviting Harry Lauder Krishnas to insert their lucky heather where it would do the most good, and Treasure straight-arming a youth in ragged imitation dogskin who attempted to relieve them of their luggage.

'You know,' she said as she scanned the store-franchises that lined the stratoport concourse. 'I think we forgot some vital travel equipment when we packed. There we go.' She pointed to a vapour sign depicting a happy, smiling family with a how-itzer and the lettering: ARMAMENTS R US.

Armitage, for the most part, had no use for guns – being of the opinion that the possession of one didn't prevent you from being killed, it merely increased the chances of killing somebody else. Nevertheless, he thought, a guest of a country must adopt its customs, and decided that a small invest-ment in a rapid-fire micro would not go amiss.

Treasure, being on expenses, took on the aspect of a walking arsenal. Armitage looked at the pistols and electro-blades and grenades as she pulled her jacket over them, the shockrod taser hanging from her belt. 'Don't overdo it, whatever you do,' he said. 'It's a wonder you can stand up. What's that?' He indicated a stubby tube about four inches in diameter with a covered control switch, which Treasure was dropping into her jacket pocket.

'It's a smart anti-personnel device,' she told him. 'I always wanted to have a go with one of them. It's sort of a surprise.'

Surface Trauma

In a Sector 64 Smokatorium, forty thousand addicted citizens spontaneously hallucinate cancerous cells breeding in their lungs, filling and distending them to burst from their mouths in a loose, grey spongy mass. Some of these citizens will claw their own throats and stomachs to shreds as they try to claw out this crawling matter, breaking off their fingernails at the root and dislocating their fingers in the process. Others will literally cough their own lungs up in their extremis.

In transition (parareality)

(*A wrenching.*

A bursting transition from the intangible to the tangible. Cells generating from nothing . . .)

Karyn hung in the chaos of the paraspace, slick and bright and utterly defined.

And Moloch beside her, golden and blazing and bright like the sun.

«Yeah!» he shouted, tactile, coruscating subsonics streaming from his mouth. «Pretty neato or *what*?»

162

He reached out a hand, brushed her lightly on her abstract arm.

And the *power* burst from them, blazing tendrils crawling over them and entwining them. Karyn's thoughts fragmented in a surge of elemental attraction that knocked her ordinary (and Justice Department suppressed) sexual impulses into a cocked hat.

The power enveloped them and pulsed.

Later, Karyn was unable to decide whether she was relieved or disappointed that this event was interrupted. On a purely sensual level it had been, as it were, mind-blowing . . . but there was something frightening about this absolute loss of control.

But before events had time to escalate, the world exploded.

The blast threw them apart, twisting and flailing. As the shifting images of the paraspace blipped past her, Karyn concentrated on slowing and turning.

The concussion of the explosion seemed to reverberate throughout her extended universe. In the distance, the small figure of Moloch. She reorientated herself and accelerated towards him.

He floated to join her, slower, slightly less sure of himself.

«I don't think I'm going to be much good at this flying lark,» he said. «I just don't seem to have the knack. I have to think about it constantly.»

Both of them, Karyn noticed, were making absolutely sure there was no 'physical' contact between them while trying not to be too obvious about it.

«You said you cleaned yourself out before you broke into paraspace. Maybe that's it.» Moloch shrugged. «Or maybe you've just got the right stuff for this place. What was that big bang?»

163

«If you're going to hand out feed-lines like that, don't ask the straight woman.» Karyn scanned the distance from which she believed the explosion had come. «There. That speck. It came from there.»

They accelerated towards it, aware in the back of their minds that something was powering them forward from a right-angle to this particular reality.

«Y'know,» Moloch said thoughtfully as they flew, «maybe these detonations happen all the time out here . . .»

«. . . But if they don't,» Karyn finished for him, «bit odd that we happen to take the first test-run the instant it occurs. Ever get the feeling you're being used?»

They drew closer. The rippling, cancerous, mile-wide mass became distinct. Others floated lazily, farther away.

«Oh Jovus . . .» The gorge rose in Karyn's self-generated throat. «How can it live? How can something like that *live*?»

«It can't,» Moloch said. «It's abstract and alien and utterly incompatible with human terms. What you're seeing is your mind trying to fit it into those terms.» He paused for a moment. «Thank you, smartass computer system.'»

Nearer.

Most of the activity appeared to be taking place to one side of the main mass.

Nearer.

A blur of insectoid manipulators scrabbling, tearing, teasing the edges apart.

«Jovus drokk . . .» Karyn said in a small, tight voice. «It's done it. It's got through. It's made a hole.»

164

Psi Division, MC1 (Surface Trauma)

In the operating theatre, the dormant body of Karyn has been left alone: what with the disruptions affecting the city on a massive scale, every medic has been drafted into emergency duty.

Karyn's body continues to breathe slow and even. The catheter draws off drops of fluid. She has been unplugged from the dialysis machine.

On the EEG read-outs, lower functions blip, higher functions are utterly flat.

The body of Karyn begins to shudder.

From her closed eyes, tiny threads of blood run down her temple to spot the padding by her head.

The Trenches, MC1

Dredd took a lift on a Manta that was heading for Sector 19 to reinforce Judges dealing with the riots sparked by a mass delusion, which had forty thousand souls believing that their loved ones had been eaten by the demon Yog Shoggoth and replaced by simulacrums matching them in every single detail. The Manta swooped down through the Sector 17 Trenches and hovered for a moment.

The Lawmaster dropped from its hatch and hit the top of a flyover, venting its retros and shooting its shocks to prevent it bouncing. Dredd swung it around and powered along the flyover. The Manta hovered watchfully overhead for a moment, then rose out of sight.

Access routes in the Trenches were kept clear for Judges by the simple periodic expedient of driving a bulldozer through them and crushing everything in its path. The garbage accumulated, however, and the Lawmaster's progress was slowed to that of a fast run.

As Dredd rode, he scanned the dimly lit wreckage for signs of life, finding none. He remembered a previous tour of duty here, safeguarding a clean-up operation intended to exterminate the non-human vermin and relocate the human. There had been a sense of covert and crawling life, a feeling that elusive figures – far more than were ever actually caught – were watching from the shadows.

Here there were none. If there were people living here now, they were being very, very quiet about it.

Up ahead, something was burning. Dredd hit a relatively clear patch of road and accelerated. The fires resolved into guttering brands lashed to the wreckage. The items amongst them also became distinct.

The pale children of the Trenches, more than a hundred of them, had been crucified. Flat scraps of board had been nailed to their foreheads, each scrawled with an improving biblical text. Other things had been done to them.

'Jovus drokk . . .' Dredd switched in his mike. 'Control? I think I may need back-up. Something's doing some serious damage here. It looks like the work of a single individual – but if one person did it then they – '

At that point the dark and sparking shape hurled itself for him. Automatically he backhanded it to knock it to one side.

The electrical discharge blew him off his bike. He hit a small damp pile of discarded plasterboard flat on his back and with a wet crunch.

166

The figure was coming for him again, skeletally thin and slightly charred, laughing, power crawling over him.

A year before, Dredd remembered, he had seen something that called itself the Jokai. He had tracked it down to Brit-Cit, and to that city's geostationary Skyhook. There, with the help of a Detective Judge Armitage, he had finally killed it, taking out the Skyhook in the process.

His first thought was that this was a creature of the same ilk . . . but there was a difference in *presence* here. Whatever else it was, it was not an alien creature. As the thin and sparking man advanced with his happy and friendly laugh, Dredd saw that it was simply a man, power from some indefinable source filling him with some supranormal vitality.

These impressions took less than a second. Dredd pulled the daystick from his belt and swung it.

A Mega-City daystick was made of heavy weighted polyprop, a cavity inside filled with liquid alloy to prevent recoil: directing the entire force of the blow in the direction intended.

The killer went down as though pole-axed. The energy that infused him sputtered and sparked.

Dredd stood over him for a moment, then keyed in his mike again. 'Neg on that back-up, Control,' he said. 'Creep didn't give me any trouble. Everything seems to be anticlimaxes today. Run the genes and prints and give me a match.'

Parareality

The Medusa-thing was intent upon forcing back the intangible walls of the hole it had made. It seemed unaware of their presence. From within came the faint screaming of hundreds, maybe thousands.

«Okay,» Moloch said softly. «Okay, okay, okay.»

Something in his tone made Karyn look at him sharply. His eyes blazed with a vicious, pulsing red.

«Let's just take the sucker out,» he said.

He launched himself towards the Medusa-thing.

A bony claw on a length of slick tubing whip-sawed, caught him under the chin, flipping him over and knocking him back, limp and unconscious.

Other tentacular appendages caught him, wrapped around him and drew him closer while a manipulator seemingly made entirely of bony blades snickered towards him.

Halls of Justice, MC1

In Control, the operator looked at her displays and did a small double-take. Then she switched Dredd in and said, 'We've got a make on this guy of yours. You're not going to like it. I don't think you'll even believe it.'

'*Get to the point,*' the voice of the Judge growled from her speaker. '*Tell me what you got.*'

'Well, there was no joy in the files so we checked out the DNA structure – and found anomalies. A proliferation of regressive characteristics. The upshot is that nobody has DNA like that any more, nobody's had DNA like this for a couple of hundred years. So we took the time-lock off the files and trawled backward.

'Your guy matches one Albert Howard Fish. Serial killer. Bigtime so far as that went in his time – and his time was the 1930s. Serious sicko, by all accounts. Cannibalism and coprophagy were the least of it.

'He was arrested in New York State in 1934 for the abduction, murder and subsequent cooking and eating with vegetables of one 12-year-old Grace Budd six years before. This kept him in a "continuous sexual fervour", it says here.

'They found a lot of newspaper cuttings when they pulled him down, most of them referring to one Fritz Haarmann – German mass-murderer of the 1920s. After his arrest, doctors found twenty-nine needles and suchlike in the flesh around his genitals. Self-inflicted.

'He preyed on children, Dredd – over a hundred at a conservative estimate. Those were what he admitted to, anyway. He used to carry around a bag of knives, a saw and a cleaver, which he referred to as his "implements of Hell".

'Suggested motives tend to differ. Psycho reports of the time suggest that he was a latent homosexual – but that's the sort of garbage psycho reports were all full of back then. His acts did seem to give him sexual pleasure, but it was more complicated than that. He would, say, emasculate a boy out of an honest desire to save him from the temptations of the flesh, and with no intention of actually killing him – and then kill him anyway, because he might talk and ruin Fish's reputation for moral rectitude. That sort of circular thinking runs through most of his crimes.

169

'He was electrocuted on the 16th of January 1936 – and here's an interesting thing. Apparently the needles in his body shorted out the chair and half of the jail the first time they tried it.'

'That ties up with what I saw,' the voice of Dredd said. *'It also ties up with these disruptions. Maybe he's a symptom – or maybe he's the cause. Have a Tek team on stand-by. I'm bringing this creep in and I want him gone over with a tooth-comb.'*

Parareality

The Medusa-thing's appendages lunged towards him. There was nothing Karyn could do. There was no way she could help Moloch now. If she tried to help him it would simply rip her to pieces.

Ah, screw it. She dived for the Medusa-thing.

And something changed inside her.

The energising and elemental power she had felt before filled her again. Without thinking much about it, she accelerated, and she was still accelerating when she hit the main mass of the Medusa-thing head-on.

She bored into it, bursting through metal and silicon and solidified bile, bursting through abstract meat and tissue for what seemed like an eternity – and then she was in the bright chaos of the parareality, ruptured strings of quasi-organic viscera exploding behind her.

She slowed and wheeled. Looked back.

The Medusa-thing was rippling, pumping fluid from an exit wound half a mile wide. The flickering form of Moloch floated nearby, relaxed in postures of unconsciousness – and drifting towards the still-spasming blade appendage.

Karyn turned and launched herself towards him.

The blades were bare millimetres from him when she got her hands around his armpits and soared to a safe distance.

After a while, Moloch began to stir. He groaned.

«I'm still alive?» he said. «Pity. If I ever get back to my real body, I'm going to have one hell of a psychosomatic lesion.»

«How did it happen?» Karyn waved a chrome-bright hand in his face. «I thought these things were supposed to be indestructible now.»

«Yeah, well,» Moloch said. «Residual body-sense, probably. I think these constructs come direct from the subconscious, and deep down the psyche still thinks it's human.»

«Oh well,» Karyn said. «I knew there was a catch somewhere. Can we go home now?»

«I think so.» Moloch shot a glance toward the distant forms of the other Medusa organisms. «I think we'd better, before the rest of those guys take an interest. You wounded the thing, maybe mortally. I reckon the hole it made should seal up on its own and . . .

And something ripped. Something pulsed. Something gaped.

«Famous last words,» said Moloch.

An unearthly slipstream caught them, tearing at their abstract meta-skin, dragging them towards the hole.

Desperately, Karyn tried to resist. «Moloch, I think I need some help here.»

«I . . .» A look of frightened surprise appeared on

171

Moloch's glowing face. «I can't. It's like it's on my –
I *can't*.»

And then he was gone, ripped from her grasp.
The sudden loss of mass sent her spinning from the
turbulence.

The last she saw of Moloch, as she felt the
intangible tug of the Bunker pulling her out, was his
glowing, twisting form plunging into the rip.

Halls of Justice, MC1

Armitage and Steel climbed rather shakily from the
cab they had taken from the stratoport. The fifty-
kilometre ride through the arterial interways of the
mega-city had taken its toll. Quite apart from the
various piles of smoking wreckage, the result of
drivers suddenly flipping out due to the disruption,
their particular driver had refused to use the auto-
assist and had driven hunched before a little glowing
Jovus on the dash, with a maniacal grin that suggested that in a previous life he had tended towards
the wearing of a rising-sun headband and shouting:
'*Tora! Tora! Tora!*'

On the skyline, through a gap in the blocks, they
could see the Statue of Judgement, that vast edifice
in the form of a particularly fierce uniformed Judge
which loomed over the comparatively pitiful and
now-demolished remains of the Statue of Liberty.

Armitage and Treasure turned from it and gazed
up at the towering bulk of the Halls of Justice.

'Y'know,' Treasure said, a little disappointed. 'I
expected it to be way bigger than the New Old
Bailey.'

'Yeah, well.' Armitage shrugged. 'Remember that

172

these days Mega-City One and Brit-Cit pretty much cover a similar area.'

The main entrance hall was cavernous, echoing, crammed with monolithic insignia and almost deserted: this was a public access area, and few Mega-City citizens felt the need to visit the Justice Department voluntarily.

The reception desks were vacant – personnel having been redeployed to deal with the current emergency. Armitage fed his smartcard into the console and stated his business.

A speaker activated, with a human voice on the other end, as opposed to transputer-generated. 'Oh yeah. The Brits.' This in such tones of weary contempt as one would say, 'Oh, yeah, those scum.'

'Extradition clearance checks,' the voice continued. 'Arresting Judge: Dredd. He's bringing in a prisoner right now, and we expect him any minute. You'd better come up.'

'You forgot to say "missing you already"', said Armitage.

'Drokk off, funnyboy.' The speaker went dead.

'Nice telephone manner,' Treasure said.

Armitage shrugged. 'It does you good to meet such friendly open people. It broadens one.'

They clipped their Brit-Cit Justice Department IDs to their lapels and waited. Presently a set of doors slid open and a young woman of about sixteen in a Justice Academy uniform stepped through them.

'I'm Cadet McGough. You're to come with me,' she said coldly, clearly radiating a sense that even a Mega-City cadet could take out anything Brit-Cit could throw at her. She frowned at Treasure, who was wearing her WOT A DYKE LOOK LIKE shirt,

173

on the grounds that if one is representing one's city-state then there should be no question as to exactly who one is. '*You're* a Judge?'

This was not homophobia, Treasure forced herself to remember. Mega-City One Judges were celibate, tended to believe that Judges who were not were degenerates and unfit to serve, and they viewed any overt expression of sexuality with the utmost suspicion.

'That's me. Tell you what, I'll try to keep my mucky hands to myself, okay?'

'That's not what you said on the flight out,' Armitage said, sticking his tongue firmly in his cheek. 'On the flight out you said how you couldn't wait to go down the Slab and get your hands on some of that Mega-City . . .'

'Up yours, y'ole fart,' said Treasure.

'Is that an offer?' said Armitage.

'I'll have to check my sponge-bag,' said Treasure.

By this time the cadet was a rather fetching shade of beetroot. 'You're to come with me,' she repeated, her voice breaking slightly on the *me*.

'Heigh-ho,' said Treasure. 'Lead the way.'

'And watch your back,' said Armitage kindly.

In transition (The Big House)

Moloch plunged through endless black shot with crawling electrical fire. Something inside him went hot and detonated: his construct-body sheared from him, streamed away from him.

Turn the world.

A wrenching . . . and for an unknowable time he

174

was in utter darkness. No senses, no body, endless black before his eyes.

His eyes?

Residual body-sense, he thought. Remember what it *feels* like to have a body.

Cells generated and bred and cohered from nowhere with a shrieking agony. Sobbing, Moloch opened his eyes, looked down at his hands.

His hands. The meat he had inhabited since he was born. He dropped them and looked around himself.

An infinite, interlocking web of clear crystal, shimmering with refracted rainbow light. For a moment he thought that somehow he had returned to the paraspace . . . but the feeling here was entirely different. Some other level of reality, utterly devoid of associations with organic life. Something analogous to the calcine structures that support the living tissue in a bone?

He realised that he was drifting, slipping through the crystal strands as though they were nothing, and without thinking much about it slowed himself to a dead stop before consciously realising that he had regained motive control again. Typical, he thought. Why the hell couldn't that have happened when it might do any good?

For lack of anything better to do, he picked a direction at random and floated the opposite way just for the hell of it. After a while he realised that something had changed.

A razor-thin, bright, perfectly straight line dopplered to infinity on both sides through the web. As he continued, the line became thicker.

He realised eventually that this must be a two-

175

dimensional plane – or however many dimensions it took to create that impression on the level upon which he was currently operating. He had not seen it at first because he had been viewing it head-on.

There was something, he thought, slightly shaky with the logic, there – but drokk it. He had had it up to his abstract neck with para-this and meta-that and quasi-the-other.

He accelerated. The plane expanded under him, vast and flat and bright.

What he had first taken, when he first saw them, to be impurities of some sort on the surface sprang into focus – and he stared at it in shock.

A vast, childish, scrawled drawing of a house. The lower section of it partially obscured by a frenzied crayon scribble.

And he had seen it before, in a dream two days before the disruption hit and he had flipped out. Exactly as it appeared here.

Upon waking, he had spent a couple of painstaking hours transcribing the image etched on his memory in almost microscopic detail – producing, ultimately what merely looked like a child's scrawl.

A precog? But the whole point about precognitions was you just got them, they were part of the world in which you lived and breathed. You didn't have to faff about with dreams . . .

Moloch changed course and swept towards the house in a tangential arc. As he drew nearer, faintly, he heard a susurration, the babbling of a thousand voices:

'. . . black shadow. I'm afraid of the shadow. It's a big black . . .'

'. . . it *now!* Give me some! Staple my arm and . . .'

'. . . Miller, right? Yeah, very cold. And then, yeah, they deserve it, but . . .'

Some of the voices sounded like children, some like adults; some like women, some like men. Some of them sounded like nothing on earth.

He drew closer. One of the windows, the window directly before him, began to expand. Bigger and bigger and bigger until there was nothing but the window.

Halls of Justice, MC1

In the end, of course, the timing was just bad enough that it was a total disaster for everybody. As the cadet led Armitage and Steel through the corridors toward the maximum security holding pens to view the incarcerated Thead, they ran into a now markedly limping Dredd shoving a cuffed and dazed killer ahead of him. The killer seemed shrunken in on himself now, the power that sustained him having all-but left him. A huge and purple bruise disfigured the side of his head. He was dressed in paper coveralls.

'Wotcha, laughing boy,' Armitage waggled a hand. 'We missed you.'

'Oh drokk,' Dredd growled, recognising him. 'It would have to be *you*, wouldn't it.' The two Judges had worked together under duress a year before, but there was no love lost between them, one holding the other to be a trigger-happy fascist, the other holding that the one was a degenerate little better than the criminals he caught.

177

'Seems that secure travel to Brit-Cit has been suspended,' Dredd growled to Armitage. 'You just stay out of my way until you can take the creep and drokk off back where you came from, you got me?'

'Charming,' said Armitage.

At this point the killer made his move. The needles in his flesh sparked with a *Raak*, pinhole-burning through his coverall. With a surge of inhuman power he wrenched his hands apart, shattering the cuffs as if they were nothing.

The killer swung a hand, hitting Dredd with a force that lifted him off his feet and slammed him into the wall. The killer made a break for it, his face calm and intent, as though concentrating upon a particularly interesting puzzle, heading directly for Treasure Steel.

Dredd flung himself after him. 'Stop the drokker!'

'You got it, matey.' Steel pulled the shockrod she had bought earlier that day from her belt and thumbed the switch.

The killer ran into Treasure with a thump, slowing him for a vital split-second so that Dredd collided with him also.

It was at this exact point that the shockrod discharged. Fifty thousand volts and an amperage designed to stun or disable rather than kill.

The charge arced through the needles in the killer's flesh, crawled over them and enveloped all three.

Opened a gateway.

The Big House

An airy room walled with seamless rose-shot marble, hung with ornate tapestries of shimmering silk. Deep-red carpeting upon the floor. Tissue-thin muslin canopies trailed to a massive, carved, oaken four-poster piled high with plump feather pillows.

The colours were bright – far too bright somehow, and glowing. Moloch realised that he was seeing visual purple for the first time since he was a child.

A small girl sat on the bed in a flowing pink gown, her back to Moloch, playing with a gilded wooden cup and ball. As she played she sang the same snatch of song over and over again: 'Here comes a candle to here comes a candle to here comes a candle to . . .'

Moloch glanced behind him, half-expecting to see a scrawled crayon drawing of a window. Instead: a heavy-leaded window of stained glass depicting a bucolic and highly-romanticised countryside. No way out through it.

Moloch floated towards the girl, realised he was floating and fell to the floor with a heavy thump.

'Here comes a candle to,' sang the girl, 'here comes a candle to here comes a candle to here comes a candle to . . .'

'It's no use talking to her,' a voice said from off to one side. 'There's nobody inside her. There's nobody inside *any* of them.'

Moloch looked around. A door in the wall had appeared from nowhere: heavy and wooden and carved with vaguely Celtic designs, it looked as though it had been there forever.

Standing in the doorway, a girl of maybe sixteen

179

in black jeans and a T-shirt. A worn leather jacket was slung over her shoulder and gripped by a negligent hand.

Her hair was black and long and tangled, braided here and there with scraps of tarnished jewellery. Scrawled across her shirt in red, warped slightly by the swell of a minimal chest, the legend: BOX BOX BOX.

'Um . . .' Moloch tried to think of something to say. He was damned if he was going to say 'Where am I?'

'Do you live here?' he settled on lamely.

The girl grinned. 'I know this place. I live here. I know every room and every door and every corridor and crack in the ceiling. It's the Big House.' And there was something dangerous in her smile. 'I live here. I'm Lucy Too.'

The Bunker

In the Bunker, in her borrowed cybernetic flesh, Karyn frantically scanned the consoles. Again, the abstract displays were meaningless, but she felt chilly knowledge slide into her head.

The Medusa-thing had opened a hole, and the hole was in a host, and that hole was going to keep on widening until it was wide enough for the Medusa organisms to burst through. From the paraspace. Into the physical universe.

They would take available matter and transmute it, reforming the Earth and all on it into their own image.

Karyn tried to question the Bunker, tried to locate

the host . . . but with sick and growing certainty she knew that she *knew* where the host was. She knew.

The host was currently lying flat on its back in an operating theatre in Psi Division. It was her own body.

INTERLUDE

A Sudden Arrival (A Tale of Old New York)

So I am sitting in Lindy's with a plate of pickled pigs'
cheeks, which are very fortifying for the blood, when
who walks in but Barry the Badger. Now, I do not
want you to think that I am incongenial, being a guy
who is known both far and wide as polite and cour-
teous to all, but Barry the Badger is a quick man with
an unkind word when he has a load on, and I do not
feel the need for unkind words at my time of life, so I
give him the very smallest of hellos when he sits at my
table and commences to tuck into my pickled pigs'
cheeks to settle, so he says, a nervous stomach.

Barry the Badger gets his name from being a
noted proponent of the Badger Game a while back
in the bad old days of prohibition, and if you do not
know the ins and outs of the Badger Game I will
recount it to you now.

It seems that a guy will be walking along and
thinking of nothing much, when a beautiful doll will
quite by chance bump into him, or drop a lace
hankie in his path, or mistake him for a guy she
knows. I hear tell of one doll going to the lengths of
flinging herself under a cab – but since this knocks
out half of her teeth and breaks both of her legs she
is not so very beautiful any more.

183

Anyway, the guy and this very beautiful doll talk of this and that, maybe over a glass of something in a little speak she hears tell of, during which she lets slip that she is the ever-loving wife of a thoroughgoing piker, who is also very jealous, who might shower her with diamonds and pearls and suchlike but never gives her any actual ready folding stuff for her own simple needs. It is a crime, she says, that there is her husband away on business in Miami, and here is she with an apartment full of the family jewels, none of which are very nutritious to eat.

So naturally, out of the goodness of his heart, the guy feels it is only right to appraise these family jewels. They repair to the apartment and they are in the midst of appraising them when Barry the Badger arrives, unexpectedly, home from Miami.

'How dare you trifle with the family jewels of my ever-loving wife!' cries Barry the Badger, waving a Betsy which he fully intends to use. 'I have a mind to shoot you like the dirty low-down dog that you are!'

The guy who, as it happens, has his own ever-loving wife and maybe any number of darling blue-eyed kids at home, says: 'Do not shoot! I am merely appraising your family jewels as a personal favour to this poor woman who is without the wherewithal to meet her simple needs and, besides, my ever-loving wife and my darling blue-eyed kids would never forgive me if I died, and would probably end their days in the gutter!'

Barry the Badger, who is a kindly man at heart unless he has a load on, is touched by this heartfelt plea and relents. And out of gratitude the guy will promptly make a present to him of all the folding stuff he has on him, and like as not more besides.

So that is how Barry the Badger gets his name and, he says, it is a good living at that, until the doll in question, one Mary Malloy, meets a certain guy and falls hopelessly in love . . . but this is a story I will tell you later.

Barry the Badger finishes off my pickled pigs' cheeks and calls to Lindy for more.

'Why, Barry,' says I pointedly, 'your nervous stomach must be exceedingly upset this evening.'

'Yes,' says Barry the Badger. 'My nervous stomach is exceedingly upset. I have just this last minute received a nasty shock. I will tell you about it.'

As you know (says Barry the Badger) since my Mary runs off with this big-shot Hollywood actor, I am hitting the sauce more than somewhat. So much so that I will sometimes see green lizards riding bicycles and will have to take the rest cures at Belview. And as you know things go from not so good to worse until I am reliant upon the kindness and generosity of strangers for my modest sustenance.

It is while I am waiting in a certain alleyway I know of, back of Maxie's off 42nd, for a suchlike individual that I am witness to the event I will now recount. I am, as I say, mulling over the possibilities of meeting with some kindly philanthropist, when something explodes behind me.

My first thought is that there is some pressure currently on Maxie's of which I am hitherto unaware, and that it will be best for all concerned if

185

I find some cover straight away – though the fact that this explosion has knocked me off my feet and deposited me neatly behind some trash cans seems already to have done the job, at that.

When I can see straight again, I see this character standing stark naked a little to the left of the spot where I previously stand.

He is on fire, and burning with a blue flame. He is screaming.

'My God, why hast thou forsaken me!' he is screaming.

I do not remember much after that, until I wake to find myself alone in the alleyway. I am a little bruised and beat-up, but there does not seem to be much else wrong with me except for an exceedingly nervous stomach condition that you remark upon before.

'Well,' I says to Barry the Badger, 'I would never dare to call such a fine, upstanding individual as yourself a liar, but it strikes me that there is something of the green lizards on bicycles in what you say.'

'I do not,' says Barry the Badger with considerable dignity, 'touch a drop since last Wednesday, being as you know somewhat short of the ready funds of late.'

And there is nothing for it but he must take me in person to the scene of this event. As I am in nothing but eating money myself at this time, and subsequently do not have a lot on, I agree to this proposal and we repair to said alleyway back of Maxie's off 42nd.

For myself, I see nothing but a few scorch-marks,

and I am about to say as much to Barry the Badger when there is an explosion exactly like the one he describes.

The next thing we know, there are two new people in the alleyway back of Maxie's off 42nd. One is dressed in leather and a helmet like the motorcycle cops you sometimes meet out of state – though he looks like no motorcycle cop I have ever seen, at that, and does not in fact have a motorcycle.

The other is a black doll in clothes like a dock worker and looking too much like a man for my taste, though I can see that under her leather jacket she is quite a looker, even though she is a dinge.

'What the drokk do you think you're doing?' this guy says to the doll – and I am here to tell you that if I ever hear this voice outside my humble abode I will not even stop to pack.

The black doll seems slightly put-out by this. 'Give it a rest, Dredd,' she snarls in a voice that sounds like the English dolls you used to meet on the tubs. 'Just leave it, okay. We're stuck together so let's just do the job, yeah?'

With that, the black doll and the motorcycle cop without a motorcycle depart from the alley at great speed.

I look at Barry the Badger. Barry the Badger looks at me.

'Well,' says Barry the Badger. 'I think it is time for another rest cure.'

'And I think I shall be joining you,' says I. 'It seems this nervous stomach of yours is exceedingly catching.'

SLICE 5

Coming Together

Parareality (Halls of Justice, MC1)

The Medusa regarded the slowly dilating hole – not the rudimentary, almost mindless impulses of the individual cell-organisms clustered about it and basking in its energy, but the single entity that lived in them all, the thing that spread Itself through the parascape, the sum of Its discrete parts. The thing that was both infinite and eternal and hungry for the world.

The Medusa.

The individual cells would not yet penetrate the hole. The thought hadn't entered the primitive structural ganglions that served in the office of neurons. The Medusa was controlling Itself, holding them back.

It had, in the past, a number of times made the mistake of pushing a part of Itself through a gateway before it was fully dilated, had watched as the gateway ruptured, collapsed into itself, forcing It to begin the whole long process of opening again.

The hole, now, was wider than it had ever been – but at most only one or two of Its individual cells might be able to burst through before the host tore itself apart. Better to wait until it was as open as possible – and then the Medusa would send Its whole self through . . . billion upon billion of Its cells into the hot bright physical world, expanding and reforming, cohering, sinking black claws into the sun.

It wouldn't be long now. It . . .

Something was wrong.

The Medusa turned Its attention to one of the cells floating before the gateway, and sensed that there was something other *behind it now, sensed that the minuscule physical organism that carried the gateway inside it was in danger, vulnerable.*

If its fellow meat-things recognised what it was, they would kill it. The host must be protected.

It could feel the resonances of these meat creatures in the hot, bright world . . . and two in particular, handily close by the host. One of them half-mad with grief and suggestible. The other . . .

The other was the nearest thing the Medusa had ever felt to Itself, and mind so similar that even across the gulf of worlds, the Medusa could take some measure of control.

In an office on Floor 50 of the Hall of Justice, Sela Kane sat staring blankly at the wall. She had simply switched off. She felt nothing.

The awful search through the cooling dead to find her son had broken her. When she had attacked Thead, only to be slapped down by Dredd, she had felt perfectly calm, and wondered why her body insisted on shrieking. It was a simple, considered and reasonable decision: she had calmly decided, as a matter of simple fact, that there would be two deaths. First Thead's, and then her own.

190

She had been left here to await the end of this current emergency, when there would be time spare to debrief her. She had been left alone and unsupervised and told to prepare some notes.

It occurred to her that Thead was still in the holding pens. And with the current emergency, there would be no more than minimal manpower to maintain security.

Without thinking much about it, and perfectly calmly, Sela Kane climbed to her feet and left the office.

Absolom Leviticus Thead squatted at the end of his holding pen bunk, perched on the frame. The straitjacket pinning his arms to his chest gave him a hulking, top-heavy appearance but he remained motionless, perfectly balanced.

He was watching, with interest, a large bluebottle as it spiralled lazily in front of him.

The fly landed on the tiled floor, meandered towards him. Thead launched himself from the bed and landed on his face, shattering his front teeth and springing his jaw.

He didn't notice. He sucked at the squashed fly.

And then, without a fuss, he sat up.

A straitjacket is intended to secure violent cases, to keep them from harming themselves. Thead squatted with his back to the bedframe, used it to pull the buckle up. His hands slipped free. He pulled the straitjacket over his head.

He walked to the door and peered out of the porthole. A corridor, cell doors.

Thead leant back against the wall and waited for

191

someone to open the door. And, after a number of hours, somebody did.

The Big House

She was strung up with razor-wire, wrists slashed in crosses, flesh hanging in flaps. Her head was thrown back and her throat was a gaping, ragged hole.

Blood sheeted from her, pooling in a catchment basin sunk into the damp concrete floor. Lead pipes ran to the walls, and somewhere he heard the sound of pumping.

A thick rubber tube hung from the ceiling, pumping blood into her upturned, open mouth.

'That's the Bloody Woman,' Lucy Too said. 'She's quite new.'

Moloch backed out of the room, shuddering, and walked down the corridor: patchwork lumps of wood nailed crazily together, rattling in the wind, bright light shining through the cracks. Lucy Too followed.

Moloch was beginning to have a vague idea of where he was, now. He was inhabiting someone else's brain, inhabiting and moving through its basic structure – and this structured hallucination of a house was merely his own identity's way of interpreting it, of imposing some order so he could function. Another person might have imagined that he or she was inside, say, anything from some complex machine to a sinking ship.

He was thinking about the personality fragments he had met. He was trying to remember what he knew about multiple personalities. He knew that when children suffer sustained abuse they can sometimes create a totally new *person* to handle it, to

192

take the pain and lock it away, to keep the core identity intact.

But multiple personalities are created by abuse over an extended period of time – and the Medusa-thing had attacked only recently. It couldn't account for the sheer size of the House.

'Did things – happen?' he asked Lucy Too cautiously. 'Did things happen to *make* these people? Do they sometimes take control and move in the world outside?'

Lucy Too shook her head. 'It's the other way round. They're not alive, they're like masks. I can put them on, and take them off, and put them away again. There's just me here.'

She paused for a moment, thoughtful. 'There was a girl who used to come here once. She could do it, too. She was Other. She had red hair. She hasn't been here for a long time, though.'

She suddenly looked up at him, peered into his eyes. 'You're Other, too,' she said. 'You're from the world outside, from Farover. I can feel masks in *your* head, just like the masks here.'

She waved a hand to indicate the doors lining the corridor. 'Most of them have been here forever – since the Birth – but sometimes the House makes new ones, sometimes they come on their own.'

'But you're not like them,' Moloch said.

'I've been here forever. I can go everywhere.' A predatorial grin. 'I can go to the Core, and one day I'm going to eat it.' She was suddenly child-serious. 'Not now though. The whole House is in danger now. We have to help it.'

'What?' Moloch said.

'There was the shaking,' Lucy Too said. 'And then

the *change*, and then you came. A lot of it was damaged. A lot of the masks got out of their rooms.' Lucy Too pointed downwards. 'There's something living here now. Down in the Cellars, filling the masks with its lifelight and twisting them, making them *eat* each other . . .

'The House is tearing itself to pieces, and when it collapses we're going to die.'

Terminal Shock

And in the hydroponic vats of Sector 28, that vast farm-belt that supplies a quarter of the city with munce and cultured fungus, inert cultures spontaneously generate human limbs and facial features. A thousand soft-tissue mouths gibber in a structured and self-consistent language that has never been heard before and will never be heard again.

New York 1936

Dredd and Treasure wandered through the strange crowd, all of whom appeared to be wearing animal or vegetable products of varying kinds, most of whom seemed to be smoking, or drinking from bag-wrapped bottles or committing acts of public indecency.

They had realised that, somehow, they were in the past – and knew, by way of Dredd checking his communications equipment, that this was long before Judges had appeared in any way, shape or form. His two-way link with Control was relaying a rather tinny version of *Felix Kept on Walking*.

'This could be what's causing the disruptions in

Mega-City,' Dredd mused grimly. 'First this Albert Fish ripped from his timeline, now us here – Grud only knows what the knock-on effect could – '

'And what have we here?' said a voice. It took Treasure a moment to place it: basic Brit-Cit English with an Irish accent – but without the *Jeyzus* and *Begorrarry* that predominated in 2116, when the Emerald Isle had become a single huge theme-park.

The owner of the voice was an official of some kind: of the blue stuff and peaky hatted and brass buttoned variety. A fat and vicious face flowering with an ethanol bloom.

While the crowd passed by, said official looked them up and down negligently swinging what appeared to be a prototype Justice Department daystick.

'And just *where* do you think you're taking this mad feller,' the official asked Treasure. 'Can't think of *anywhere* on forty-second that would want your sort.'

The automatic and implicit racialism prevalent in this time went over Treasure's head. It took a second for the meaning of his words to sink in.

'And what,' she said in a tight, controlled voice, 'exactly do you think I am?'

The official grinned insinuatingly. 'I know what you are, Sambo; it's more a question of how much you want to pay me to – '

But Treasure had had enough. Before the official could react, she straight-armed him in the gut, and as he bent double with a *whuff* of expelled air, uppercutted him to knock him back, following through to catch his nose with her elbow.

The official went down with a small spray of blood

and a *rak* of broken cartilage. The passers-by suddenly feigned an absolute uninterest in the scene.

Dredd was furious. 'What the drokk to you think you're playing at, Steel?'

'You wouldn't understand.' Treasure was breathing heavily. 'I think we'd better leg it. Oh for drokk's sake, Dredd. Run!'

Halls of Justice, MC1

'Drokk me!' Armitage exclaimed. 'You're taking the whiz.'

The Tek-Judge shrugged. 'That's what it sounds like. One or two minor variations, but it sounds like a time-flare.'

'Yeah, right,' said Armitage. 'And maybe the Luciferge and all his little evil pixies spirited them away. Time travel is impossible.'

They were in Chief Judge McGruder's office, where Armitage had been describing the events prior to Dredd, Steel and the killer's disappearance. Now the Chief Judge nodded thoughtfully from behind steepled fingers. Armitage thought he could detect a hint of five o'clock shadow on her craggy face.

'We've known about time travel for some time now,' she said. 'It's classified information. We know so little of the nature of time that unsanctioned experimentation could be disastrous – but since your assistant probably has first-hand knowledge of it now, whenever she is, I see little point in keeping the fact of its existence from you.'

Armitage thought about this. 'Okay. So they could be anywhere in history. Sort of a big place to search, don't you think, the whole of history?'

'It's not quite as bad as that,' the Tek-Judge said. 'I mean, it sounds like this Albert Fish guy converted the power in a shockrod. That's not all that much. That gives us maybe one hundred, two hundred years tops. My guess is point of origin, temporally at least.'

'And anything and everything they do is going to change history,' said Armitage. 'The world we know and inhabit will never have existed.'

'We don't believe it works like that,' McGruder said.

We?, thought Armitage. He remembered the story of a certain British despot from the late twentieth century, who had been the single most prominent cause of the tensions which would later explode into the Civil War, and whose barking clinical insanity had taken the overt form of addressing herself in the Royal 'We'. Oh Grud, he thought, don't tell me Mega-City's Chief Judge is flipping out, too. That's all we need.

'. . . correct me if I'm wrong,' said Chief Judge was saying, 'but *our* reality, our *now*, won't be affected any more than your Lawmaster will be affected simply because a street you passed through an hour back gets bombed.'

The Tek-Judge nodded. 'That's near enough. Although,' he added thoughtfully, 'if it were a *big* enough bomb it could take out the whole *lot*. Maybe that's what . . .'

Armitage would never know exactly what the Tek's theory was, because at that moment the intercom on the desk started bleeping frantically.

The Chief Judge hit the switch. 'McGruder.'

'This is Mahler,' a worried voice said. 'Max Security Holding. We have an escape.'

They arrived at the holding cell to find the uniformed Mahler interrogating a battered, wiry woman with a fresh bruise flowering on her temple.

'. . . know why,' she was saying. Armitage looked into her eyes and saw fresh pain and grief – but this was overlaid by the shock of one who has found herself doing something without the faintest idea of why.

'I just don't remember thinking at *all*,' she said miserably. 'It wasn't even that I wanted to kill him. Not really. It was just like I *knew* he was here and I had to go to him.'

Armitage glanced around at the cell, then gestured towards the straightjacket lying discarded in a corner. 'He was wearing this?'

'No.' The woman spoke vaguely, repeating something she had obviously run over a number of times before. 'I went in, and he was waiting behind the door, and he hit me. It wasn't like he knocked me unconscious. It was like there was something else . . .' She lapsed into silence.

'What we need,' said McGruder, 'is some hard evidence – and with the Psi Division out of it, that just leaves the psychoprobe.'

Armitage, meanwhile, was feeling oddly sympathetic towards the wiry woman – who was, he gathered, an undercover Judge. She had obviously suffered some recent, deep and absolute trauma, and he knew from certain experiences – experiences which must for the moment remain classified – how possible it was for the entirely innocent to fall under some intangible but pervasive control. Besides, the use of the psychoprobe (the technology of which had never been refined due to the ready supply of psis who could in ordinary circumstances perform its function more quickly and simply) was known and feared throughout the more relaxed city-states as the barbarous instrument of torture it truly was.

'Oh no you don't,' he said to the Chief Judge, with an angry belligerance more feigned than actual. 'This woman here is responsible for you losing my prisoner – and I'm damned if I'm going to let her out of my sight for one minute.'

Halls of Justice, Psi Division MC1

The animal moved through the corridors, unthinking, unnoticed, operating entirely on the lymbic system, the mammalian brain. The animal brain.

For Its own part, the Medusa had no comprehension of physical structures in more than the most abstract sense. It was simply aware of the pulsing gateway ahead of It, a series of planes and obstacles which must be negotiated. It squatted in the brain stem, guiding Its host, cloaking it in an electrostatic field which disrupted the flow of information between the visual cortex and temporal lobes of any nearby organism.

Occasionally It would allow the animal to feed – and the only reaction of its victims as it punched fingers into their soft abdomens, pulled internal organs out with bulged, hooked fingers, was one of blank surprise. Even as they died their attacker had no reality for them.

The host-body of the gateway was close now,

199

overhead. It walked through the corridors and climbed the stairwells, taking the most direct route, unthinking, unnoticed. Like a ghost.

And, eventually, It reached Its destination.

The woman lay motionless, tubes and leads trailing from her. Her red hair had been shaved.

The body that had once been Absolom Leviticus Thead pulled the tubes from her and picked her up. Her body was warm, boiling almost, and the Medusa perceived that inside her the gateway was huge now. It carried the woman out into the corridor, blood and saline running from the tubes in a thin trail.

An alarm was shrilling. Two meditechs ran past It without a second glance. It heard their shocked babbling.

It walked back the way It had come, a ragged, bloodstained man in the remains of holding-pen coveralls, the woman hanging from his arms. Nobody noticed him. Nobody saw.

Now It would have to find a safe place for her. Now It would have to go to ground.

New York 1936

They pelted through the streets, the sound of whistles fading behind them. Soon they found themselves lost. The streets were deserted here: this was an area of warehouses and waterfront, closed down for the night.

The distant sound of the city, the lap of the water, the groan of iron structures in the icy wind, made Treasure nervous. She jumped when Dredd's motion-detector began to bleep.

There was the sound of gunfire nearby.

Cautiously, they made their way around the brick walls of a warehouse, found themselves looking upon a makeshift and rotting wooden wharf.

Two automobiles of an archaic, canopied design were parked here at skewed angles, their headlamps illuminating the scene.

Dark, suited figures were lining a group of figures similarly dressed but handcuffed and in hoods which covered their faces, against a pitted, bloodstained warehouse wall. The first group carried what Treasure thought of as assault rifles of some kind – though the circular magazines clipped to them seemed vaguely impractical to her.

Several other figures already lay sprawled and jerking, their pumping blood bright scarlet in the illumination from the headlamps.

The figures with the guns stepped back and worked the loading mechanisms with a ratcheting clack. They took aim at the figures lined against the wall, talking and laughing amongst themselves as though simple workmates in some repetitive job of work.

And then there was a shout.

A ratty, slightly ragged man in a sloppy jersey and a cap, who had been sitting on the mudguard of one of the cars and smoking something, called to his fellows, and waved a hand in the direction of Treasure and Dredd.

The rattle of machine-gun fire. Dredd and Treasure hauled themselves back as slugs tore at the corner of the warehouse.

Terminal Shock

And in the Happy Daze resettlement block, Judges Turner and Brosnan are investigating a garbled emergency call from one Judge Nail: Judge in need of assistance.

At some point in the past the lock has been broken and mended inexpertly. The door gives easily.

Brosnan slaps at the light switch beside the door. 'Dead,' he says. 'The lights are – oh Jovus. That smell. What's that smell?'

'Spoiled meat,' Turner says. 'Don't jump to conclusions. It's probably coming from the refrigerator.'

Turner pulls a torch from her belt and together they work their way through the broken and overturned furniture. Occasionally, a draught from the open window catches the grimy sheet polymer over the windows and sets it rattling.

'This place is a mess,' Turner says. 'I think there was some serious violence happening here.' The flashlight plays over the wall. 'You see those? Scattergun pellets.'

'What's that stuff around them?' Brosnan says. 'It can't be blood . . .'

Turner chips a shred of ichor from the wall with the nail of a little finger, examines it. 'It's still greasy, like ear wax. Leave it for the bright boys in Forensic. I think we – '

Something thumps behind one of the doors leading off from the room.

Silently, Turner indicates the door. Brosnan nods and crosses over to it, presses himself back against the wall beside it, Lawgiver drawn.

He eases the door open, then darts through it.

'*Armed Judge! Make a move and I make a* hole *and . . . oh, Oh Grud. Oh Grud I . . .*'

His voice is bemused, vacant.

'*Brosnan?*' *Turner runs to join him.*

The smell of rotting meat is overpowering. In one corner of the kitchen there is a small, neat pile of bones. All that is left of the body is the torso, remains of an upper arm hanging from it by a string of tendon.

Judge Nail is gnawing on the armpit, shreds of skin and flesh hanging from the remains of his teeth.

'*Eating,*' *he is muttering happily.* '*Meeting eating meeting meat . . .*'

The Big House

Lucy Too led him down through the House: along creaking patchwork corridors and catwalks, across vast brick vaults with chessboard floors; down rusting iron staircases and through massive oak doors; through halls hung with shredded membrane, through the false backs of cupboards and through secret passages, through skylights set into the floors and into whole new networks of corridors.

The House was vast, unending, and every wall was full of doors.

Some were splintered, hanging off their hinges, those behind them escaped or rotted to greasy stains. Without their inhabitants to give them life, the rooms themselves had deteriorated: simple boxes of cracked plaster and bare floorboards.

Other doors, when opened, showed interiors larger than was physically possible, whole landscapes. A hall hung with broken kites, flame leaping from one to the other; a gallery of portraits stretching to infinity; a black ironclad battleship floating over a crippled stone circle, blue light blazing from its ports; a room full of statues, stone women hung with jewels . . .

They went down.

A corridor lit with bright and flickering neon, an endless stream of figures shuffling out from one door and into another in the opposite wall. Their faces were perfectly smooth.

Lucy pulled him back.

'We can't go that way,' she said. 'We just *can't*.' There was barely-suppressed terror in her voice.

They backed away and found an elevator shaft, spiderclimbed the cables. Out into a dark corridor, smelling like a ruptured sewer, fleshlike fungus clotting the walls.

Moloch began to feel a growing pressure: vague images of decay, a memory of a stump that talked.

The House had degenerated here, walls cracked and flaking, paper thin – and somehow he knew that there was *nothing* on the other side.

Animals lived here. Fleshy sacs of gas, sculling through the air with pale and elongated claws; flayed lumps of meat and gristle, interlocking, thinking worms inside them; a stream of warm and luminescent gas . . .

'Little Sisters of the Goddess,' Lucy Too said. 'We're getting close now. We're over the Cellars.'

She pulled back a door, the wood crumbling under her hands.

A lead-lined cubicle, ruptured pipes hanging from the walls, slick water oozing from them and spattering to the fractured tile below. A door in the far wall.

A girl was slumped here, giggling, legs splayed out in front of her, a midnight blue dress hitched up around her waist.

She looked up at them. She was eyeless: just black, bloody holes. Maggots moved under her skin.

'That's Baby Blue,' Lucy Too said. 'She's harmless.' She walked to the inner door and pulled it open.

Light burst from the doorway. The roar of machinery, the smell of smoke. The floor under their feet began to shake, to fracture. Lucy Too clung to the door-frame, her feet slipping from under her. With a cry she dropped out of sight.

Moloch dived through the door. A cavern, walls sloping sharply to a sheer drop, Lucy Too dropping to the rocky floor a hundred metres below, arms flailing.

Moloch swooped towards her, got under her, took hold of her and pulled her upward. She clung to him, breathing quick and ragged, warm heart hammering against his side.

It was only then that he realised he had been flying as though in the paraspace.

Stone ribs radiated from a hole in the centre of the cavern, blazing with a rippling golden light inside.

'That's the way into the Cellars,' Lucy Too said. 'The Cellars are down there, through the Trapdoor.'

'The light . . .' Moloch said.

'The lifelight,' she said. 'Spilling out of the core. When it fills the house, the masks will eat and eat and eat each other and tear the House down.'

Between the stone ribs the floor of the cavern was *alive*: wet, grey creatures squirming together, thrashing, eating each other. Grey snakes struck at pseudo-lizards swallowing them whole; a mantis the size of a dog lunged viciously at the slumped, boneless body of a beached jellyfish.

Slim copper stilts rose from the rippling grey mass to a complicated clockwork machine squatting directly over the pit. A jointed metal arm hung from its base, a jagged iron claw clenching and unclenching.

The claw reached down into the pit, tearing at the light as though it were a tangible thing. Above the chatter and clatter of the mechanism, over the seaswell sound of the rippling grey creatures, Moloch thought he heard something small screaming.

The claw reared and plunged, reared and plunged, shreds of congealed light hanging from it.

Moloch floated for the machine, Lucy Too clinging to his shoulder, saw as they got closer that there was a cage inside the machine, a hulking form within, indistinct behind the bars, pulling at levers and turning handles frantically, gurgling gleefully to itself.

It saw them. Looked up at them, the controls dropping from its hands. The mechanical claw splashed flaccid into the pool of light.

It opened the door of the cage, climbed on top of it. Its hands were pale, each the size of a human torso.

Its face was skeletal, paper-white ulcerated skin stretched across a bulging skull. Its ears and nose had been pulled off, leaving bloody flapping sockets.

Its hair was sparse and stringy, caked with clotted yellow pus.

One eye was missing, just a grey and twisted weeping cord hanging from a socket. The other was bulbous, the lid pulled back and stitched. A claw sprouted from its head, counter-weighted, one talon broken to expose soft veins in its hollow. Its mouth . . .

A single jagged tooth a foot long – gouges in its chest, old scars. Soft, wormlike tendrils hung from its mouth on either side.

It lunged for them with a gurgling roar, leaping more than twenty feet. Moloch surged backwards, as its huge pale hands flashed before their eyes.

Lucy Too was struggling against him and babbling: 'It's Hollowhead! It's Hollowhead! He wants to pull it out and pull it out and see what's *inside*! It's Hollowhead and I . . .'

Moloch accelerated for one of the rocky spurs that radiated from the pit, dropped her there and turned, flung himself into the air again. The creature had leapt from the machine now, was heading towards him through the writhing grey creatures. Its legs were atrophied, trailing behind it; it dragged itself by its hands.

'Imp guano tub gi yob,' it said, a hot and clotted voice. 'Imp giant tub eel yule op an speed yule ufo an premeditate up clutted hubby semen . . .'

Moloch flew towards it, accelerating. It reared before him. A hand came up and swatted him away like a fly.

Terminal Shock

Cutting through the West 75 interCit Terminal, Lewis Creed, thirty-five, married with two children, noticed a figure curled asleep on a bench . . . and found himself wondering, purely hypothetically, what would happen if he stuck a finger in the derelict's eye.

There was no emotion attached to the thought, none at all. It was like the times he stood on the mono, watching a girl, imagining how her teeth would break and how he would smear the blood over her as he did her . . .

He strolled closer to the bench, the smell of piss and sweat.

The derelict was maybe sixty years old, maybe older, sprawled like a puppet with its strings cut. Stringy white hair coming loose from a pale scalp, a pus-encrusted sore on the temple. Decomposing bundles clutched to the chest.

He gurgled something as Creed knelt beside him. His teeth had rotted to his gums. Creed reached out a tentative hand.

Bursting through the cornea and the gelid membrane of the lens into warm mucus, the feel of the optic nerve against his fingertip like a uteral opening in miniature.

Creed increased the pressure, sunk his finger to the third joint. It was harder than he'd imagined, like pushing through a side of meat.

The derelict shuddered, mouth working. 'Muh,' he said softly. 'Muh. Muh. Muh . . .'

It was a long time before the body stopped shaking. Creed pulled his finger from the socket, contemplated the blood and mucus and cephalic fluid coating his finger, licked it absently.

A sudden pain in his head: hot blood pounding through fragile capillaries. Something behind him, sucking at him . . . Creed staggered to his feet. His extremities were numb now, numb and shaking, eyes were haemorrhaging. The hole opened up like some black and bloody flower and he –

Turn the world.

New York 1936

The killer walked the streets of New York all but insensate. The power that filled him, the power channelled and diverted by the needles inside himself, the power that made him strong . . . somehow, on a level he was no longer able to define, somehow the power had diminished him. It had eaten away his mind. He could remember the towering grandeur of his Faith, but it was like remembering the use of legs after one is paralysed: he simply could not do it any more.

Now he moved like an automaton, responding automatically to stimuli, and responding with complexity, too . . . but there was nothing inside him. He remembered the elaborate, spontaneously improvised rituals he had performed upon his kills, remembered how it had seemed so necessary, so right. He could feel nothing of that now.

He knew that he should feel panic, loss, betrayal at the loss of his inner self – and indeed he felt the purely physical sensations associated with these emotions – but he actually *felt* nothing.

The killer walked the streets of New York, dressed

in an overcoat he had killed for, because the naked must be clothed. Electrical energy occasionally glowed from within, and scorched the mohair.

And, at length, he found what he was looking for: a building, maybe fifty stories, in a state of partial completion; deco cladding giving way to a skeletal structure of scaffold and girders.

The vast sections of the killers's brain, the sections that had been rewired to expend all their processing power upon an intuitive grasp of interspatial relationships, noted the interplay of iron shapes, saw the coincidental, miraculous, perfection of their form.

The killer looked up and felt a surge of absolute joy, a joy that burnt out still more of himself. The needles within himself, the needles placed with such precision, had been an unconscious offering for the God that is in everything, an artifact addressed to the very structure of the universe itself.

These metal forms before him, and quite by chance, over the course of a thousand accidents of design and construction, were the same thing on a larger order of scale.

This was his place.

Halls of Justice, MC1

What with the city still in chaos, the escape of one mass-murderer, and the mysterious disappearance of another together with Judge Dredd, it was some while before anyone had the spare time to check up on the unconscious Judges in Psi Division. Once it was discovered that Karyn was missing, the alarm was raised.

The simple fact that Psis were generally mistrusted meant that the Justice Department kept tabs on them constantly: each Psi was implanted with a transponder which enabled Control to triangulate upon them and locate them with pinpoint accuracy.

'There you go,' the operator said, punching up the display.

'Oh drokk,' said McGruder. 'That's Undercity.' She glanced around the Control centre, at the operators running a decimated force as it tried to keep the lid on the city. 'We don't have the manpower to do a trawl. It's probably unrelated, anyway. She's probably just gone walkabout.'

Armitage, who for a while now had been feeling about as useful as a third leg, snorted. 'Of course it's drokking related. How many coincidences do you want to swallow in one day?'

'Oh yeah?' McGruder studied the Detective Judge thoughtfully. Earlier, when she had learnt that the Brit-Cit Judge would be arriving, she had decided to check him out. This had involved calls to the Mega-City Intelligence Division, which maintained extensive files on the world's various city-states, and a review of Dredd's report, from half a year ago, his meeting with the man. It had made interesting reading.

She came to a decision.

'Tell you what,' she said. 'You're so hot to try it, why don't you do it? You have our official sanction to search wherever you like for this guy of yours. And if you feel like some backup, why don't you take Kane with you? You're so hot on protecting her, let's see if she feels the same.'

The Undercity, MC1

It was dark here. The body that had once been Absolom Leviticus Thead sat immobile, his back against a crumbling brick wall, dormant. Beside him the woman lay sprawled, lit from within by a pale light that illuminated nothing of her surroundings.

Dark shapes moved under her skin. The hole inside her was almost fully open now.

The Medusa had withdrawn from Thead, resurfaced in the paraspace, leaving one tiny shred of awareness behind to watch over the woman. Now It infested the individual cells gathered around the hole, goaded them forward.

Somewhere in the distance, along miles of tunnels, something rattled. Thead and the woman remained motionless. In the dark.

The Big House

Moloch's head hit the wall of the cavern, and something snapped in his neck. He dropped to the floor, landing heavily, crushing grey animals – felt his head twisting at a soft and unnatural angle. And then realised that he couldn't feel anything else.

He tried to move and failed. He was paralysed from the neck down. The animals crawled softly over him, biting pieces out of him and he couldn't feel it.

Hollowhead turned and peered at him with its one functioning eye, dragged itself towards him with its huge, pale hands.

It loomed over him, blocking out the lifelight from the pit. Moloch lay in its shadow, listening to the air whistling through his mouth as he hyperventilated. He couldn't feel his lungs.

'Curtest mynas upend plans ad mu slash in supporting . . .' Hollowhead said, a trickle of warm living drool spattering into Moloch's eye. 'Raker sol manor.'

Its head opened up: skull split down the middle and peeled back jagged, clawlike, skin hanging from it in stretched and twisted strips. There was nothing inside.

Suddenly, frantically, over to one side, he heard Lucy Too shouting: 'It's a mask! It's a *mask*!' But he already knew that. The creature was a construct, animated by a bright fleck of some Core-spirit, unexisting on any real level – but on this level, in the Big House, it could kill him just as if it were . . .

And then Moloch realised what Lucy Too meant. She wasn't talking about the creature, about Hollowhead. She's talking about *me*, he thought wildly.

Before, in the parareality, his construct had been susceptible to damage because on the most basic and fundamental level he *believed* it could be. But he was a self-aware, self-referring structure with no actual presence in the physical world – and as such he wasn't constrained by it. He controlled his perceptions and controlled his form – and he could pull down any form he needed.

He repaired himself, felt his phantom neurotecture *burning* inside as it regenerated, small squirming animals falling away from him electrocuted.

He flung himself into the air as the jagged, snapping halves of head closed on the space he had occupied a fraction of a second previously.

He streaked across the cavern, slowed, hung in

the air and watched the creature smash its head into the ground a couple of times.

After a while it realised that there was nothing there. It cast around, breath rattling in the halves of its hollow head, then began crawling towards Lucy Too. It reached the rocky spur upon which she was lying and hauled itself up the side.

She backed off, desperately shoving herself back with her heels. The gap between them widened – but in the end it would make no difference. Her retreat was cut off by a solid rock wall, on either side were pits of squirming creatures who would eat her alive. There was no escape.

It was no use, Moloch thought, attacking the creature again in his present form. He tried to imagine a new body for himself, how it would *feel* to be something like the monster below.

It almost worked. He slit down the middle and curled in on himself, rubbery flesh bursting from his head. The pain was intense; he felt himself drowning in it, losing his identity in a wound that was himself.

He wrenched himself back, snapped back to the golden glowing form he had occupied in the paraspace. This was going to take some time to get the hang of – time he didn't have. Lucy Too had backed to the wall now, was screaming up at him as he floated indecisively.

He swooped towards her, restructured himself again – into the cybernetic creature he had occupied in the bunker. The tang of ozone filled his mouth. He transmuted a claw: now there was a cavernous and evil-looking blaster attachment grafted to his arm, loaded and armed – and the best part about it

214

was that since he'd never fired it before, he could make it do what he liked.

He brought the gun up and fired. White-hot plasma streamed from its snout, burning the Hollowhead's head away in a spray of vaporised meat and bone.

It didn't notice. It was still coming for them.

Moloch sliced it in half, burst the brain analogue nestling in its stomach. The two halves collapsed on either side of the rocky spur: grey creatures eating, the sound of a thousand little buzzsaws.

Moloch shifted back to his glowing paraspatial form and helped Lucy Too to her feet. She was over her hysteria now, but still white-faced and shaking.

'That thing would have killed you?' he asked her.

'No.' She shuddered. 'I'd still be alive. While the gastric juices pumped. Thank you.'

Moloch picked her up and they drifted towards the glowing pit. As they drew closer, Moloch saw things moving under the surface, feebly moving misshapen limbs and appendages.

As he watched, a severed hand clutching a huge eye broke the surface, rolled over and sank again without a trace.

'We have to go in there?' he said. 'Through that?'

'It can't hurt you,' Lucy Too said. 'It can only digest the things it made.'

'What about you?' Moloch said.

'I'll be all right, I think. I think I have my own core.'

'Well let me know if you're not,' Moloch said. 'I'll try to pull you out.'

Lucy Too nodded. He took them down into the pit.

The Bunker

A panel slid back. There was a roaring whine – and Karyn simply *knew* that inert helium was being exchanged for air. Karyn stepped into a dark, narrow gallery filled with weapons: pistols and rifles and knives, hand-held rocket launchers and grenades. Semtex. Detonators. It frightened her, for the simple reason that *somebody* had known the weapons would have to be used at some point.

She pulled a large machine pistol from a rack, turned it over in her cybernetic hands. It was archaic, like the other weapons, maybe hundreds of years old – but it had been well-oiled and kept in pristine condition by the inert atmosphere of the gallery. It would do the job.

Her body had been moved. The bunker system had tracked it. It was down here now, in the Undercity, somewhere nearby.

And the bunker had told her what to do. In the initial stages, if it was to break through, the Medusa would have to gestate its cells through the host. Kill the host and you shut down the hole.

Karyn's body was nearby. And Karyn knew she had to kill it.

New York 1936

The slugs smacked into the corner of the block. Dredd slapped Treasure on the shoulder. 'Cover me.'

Treasure tried to remember her woefully inadequate Brit-Cit combat training. She dragged from her jacket a micro-auto she had bought some hours before and hit the ground, stuck the smallest possible target-area around the corner of the warehouse and sprayed slugs on rapid fire.

One of the suited men clutched at his throat and went down. Another spun, flailing, his left shoulder exploding.

And Dredd was diving from cover, hitting the ground and rolling. Treasure kept firing as the suited men dived for the cover of their cars, picking another off.

The hooded men who were to have been the victims were now in some confusion, blundering about in panic, tripping and falling over the prone bodies of those previously shot.

The suited men were under cover now, had pinpointed Treasure and were retaliating. Bullets strafed the ground before her; she racked herself back.

A drainpipe ran down the brick wall of the warehouse. Treasure desperately hauled herself up it a couple of metres and, clinging with her feet and one hand, exposed herself again. The trick was, like first exposing herself at ground level, to appear where an opponent would not automatically expect, to win an extra couple of seconds of reaction time.

Off to one side, she saw the bulky black shape of Dredd moving in – and saw for the first time a technique that she had only ever heard about.

The Mega-Cit Judge was not taking cover: he was simply moving with a calm and fluid grace that, somehow, fitted so naturally into the world that it caused no sense of threat, nothing to draw the eye. In such a way, a man might walk calmly toward you and stick a knife in your gut and pass smoothly on before you are aware of what is happening.

Treasure only saw this because she knew what to look for – and once seen, of course, such a technique is useless. But the suited men were concentrating on *her*. Brick fragmented by her face, cutting a gouge across her right cheek – and she lost her grip on the drainpipe.

As she dropped, she saw that the dark figure of Dredd, very close now, smoothly and without a fuss, was bringing up his Lawgiver.

The explosions came almost simultaneously. The gas tanks of the cars ruptured and detonated secondarily. The suited men burned and twisted and screamed.

Dredd was picking off the survivors on single-shot.

A minute later, Treasure and Dredd looked upon the smoking wreckage. The smell of burning meat reminded Treasure of the horrors she had encountered back in Brit-Cit, in the Tight White house. She wanted to choke.

The hooded men were still stumbling through the wreckage. By sheer luck more than anything else, none of them had been more than injured by the actions of Treasure and Dredd.

'What do we do with them?' Treasure asked.

'We leave them,' Dredd told her shortly. 'They saw nothing.'

He headed back the way they had come – and Treasure saw that his bad leg was troubling him: he walked on his foot like it was made of wood, nerveless.

'Don't just stand there gawping,' Dredd said curtly. 'We have a job to do, remember. We have someone to find.'

The Big House

Solid golden light, drowning out every other stimulus. A brief flare of static electricity crawling inside him – then no sensation at all other than the feel of Lucy Too in his arms.

'Are you all right?' he said.

'I'm fine,' she said in his ear. 'Keep going.'

Shifting forms began to appear, fluctuations of brightness, becoming more solid as they descended: a child's scrawl of a bird, teeth in its beak; interlocking cones and spheres; words with a vicious life of their own.

It became harder and harder to move. The light around them became liquid; a physical, tangible thing. The forms cohered into actual unseen creatures, pressing against him, rubbing their soft bodies against him.

He felt himself losing control. He felt a scream building up inside, a struggling animal screaming to make them go away, just go away. And then Lucy Too's hands were on his face, cool and calm, snapping him back to coherence.

'They're just ghosts,' she said. 'Ghosts of eaten masks.' She took his hand in hers, pushed it to one side. 'Look over there. Look over *there*. The Core.'

A shimmering speck, dark against the blank gold light. He headed towards it, and as he drew nearer, as it became distinct, his flesh began to crawl again.

The hole was the shape of a woman, perfectly delineated, hanging asprawl in the gulf.

And Moloch recognised the shape of Karyn.

Terminal Shock

In a room hung with artificial human figures, John Michael Taylor absently manipulated the limbs of a wooden artists' mannequin into a vaguely balletic pose. It was a question of attitude, a question of posture; moving a hand through a conceptual arc, a tone of voice, pumping one pheromone rather than another.

It was simple, *life* was simple. You just supplied the correct answers, either verbally or in terms of body language and positioning.

He remembered when he was a child, the juve psychologist laying picture cards in front of him, asking him to make up a story about them. What do you see, John? Tell me what you *see*.

'There's a little girl,' he had said. 'And a man. A little girl and a man. He rescued her. She was drowning in the river and he dived in and he saved her. He's bending over her. He's giving her the kiss of life . . .'

He had been quite proud of his story.

He picked up a magazine, flicked through it until he came to a picture of a blonde woman in stockings and suspenders posing on a stile. He tore out several features and pasted them on the wooden figure: eyes and a smiling mouth, breasts.

He studied the figure for a while, then hung it with the others; dolls and puppets and plasticine figures, contorted in agony or laughter or masturbation, smiles and screams and labels scrawled and painted on them: *There's somebody in the* house *with us, there's* . . .; *Eat it* up *me; How can you move without a, how can you* move *without a head?*

220

Then he turned his attention to the thing on the bed, pulled back the polythene sheeting, examined it.

It twitched under his hand. Its eyes opened into black encrusted holes and he lurched back with a cry. Hanging puppets clattered together as his shoulder brushed them.

The thing on the bed reared up, opened its mouth. 'Want to suck,' it said. 'Want to suck and suck and *suck* and suck and suck . . .'

Taylor stared at its rotting patchwork head and something went wrong with his heart and the hole opened up and he –

Turn the world.

The Undercity, MC1 (The Bunker)

'What was that?' Armitage said. 'Did you hear that?' He cast around with his torch, the beam playing on old and fractured brick walls.

'I heard nothing.' Sela continued to trudge along, her face bone-white in the torchlight, her eyes vacant and with a bruised look about them.

Neither of them knew how long they had been down here. It might have been minutes since they found the hatch that led down into the Undercity. It might have been hours.

The hatch had been forced. Someone had come this way recently.

Armitage had gathered that the Undercity encompassed cubic miles of roofed-over ruins, and had therefore been vaguely disappointed to discover what merely seemed to be this endless twisting maze of tunnels and disused sewers. Occasionally he thought he heard voices, thought he saw ragged shapes moving through the shadows, but thus far nothing had occurred to confirm either.

And, in the back of his mind the vague feeling that he was being directed, that the tunnels were opening up and closing down and twisting in upon themselves, consciously leading him through themselves into some . . .

Lost in his own thoughts, he did not realise that Sela had stopped until he walked into her.

'Look,' she said calmly, patently uncaring whether he looked or not.

There, ahead of them, a small group of thin, pale, ragged figures. None seemed to be older than his or her mid-twenties, but each had the wizened, strangely ageless quality of those with a drastically truncated life-cycle. In the light of dimly burning torches, they squatted in a loose circle at a point where the tunnel widened slightly, sprinkling some dark powder from pinched fingers to make intricate designs on the floor. A low, murmuring, ululating chant reverberated from them.

As Armitage and Sela drew closer, the figures noticed them, scampered off startled down the tunnel and were lost from sight save for the firefly-glow of their torches.

Armitage glanced down at the designs on the floor: circuit diagrams of insane complexity, indecipherable to his limited technical knowledge. He played the light absently over the tunnel walls – found a hatch suggesting those found in a shuttle.

Silently, seemingly of its own accord, the hatch slid back to reveal a semi-circular opening in the wall of the tunnel. Pale golden light glowed from within.

New York 1936

They wandered the night streets of the city. Around them revellers in sloppy white tie and tails mingled with tough-guys in whipcord. Chorus girls on their way home or to the clubs; their poorer and more down-at-heel sisters. They passed a clump of men shooting craps on a blanket – and something about Dredd's aura must have crossed through time and cultural boundaries, because at the sight of the pair the blanket was snatched up and the group dispersed.

Limelight and Edison bulbs flashed out names refashionable in Mega-City One. Occasionally, those they passed would startle or fall back, or enquire where the fancy-dress party was, or hurl the odd deprecatory remark – but at this time of night, those on the street were in no state of sartorial judgement.

Dredd's motion detector field was extended to its maximum, constantly checking for some anomaly, some unnatural factor in the movements of those around it that might denote the unique presence of the killer. It was a long shot, but it was the only positive action they could think of.

In the end, however, and quite by chance, it was Treasure who made the breakthrough. She had grown up in a world in which a large proportion of its surface had been ripped off and flung into the air due to various wars and suchlike disturbances, a world in which the atmosphere was full of so much suspended junk that she had never seen a clear sky.

223

The starlit sky overhead was utterly alien to her, and disturbing; she felt her eyes constantly drawn to the skyline, felt her mind desperately trying to cope with it.

Dredd's iron control meant that he was untroubled by this; he concentrated utterly upon the job in hand – and thus it was Treasure who was looking up to catch the brief and almost unnoticeable flash.

'Look,' she said. 'Look up.'

Dredd followed her gaze, scanning on infra.

There, lit by ambient glow from the spotlights of other buildings, the partially completed edifice of a skyscraper, girders and scaffolding skeletal amongst its incomplete art deco facade.

And spread-eagled, balanced on the topmost girder, the tiny figure of a man silhouetted against electrical fire.

The Bunker

'Jovus. Will you look at this?' Armitage glared around him at the interior of the bunker, at the arcane, archaic consoles, at the cybernetic monstrosities on the couches. He scanned the abstract shapes streaming across a circular monitor. 'Some sort of sonar but I can't . . .'

He became aware of a broken, keening wail. His head snapped round to where Sela Kane sat curled against the curved wall of the chamber, clasping her knees and sobbing.

She broke off and was still. 'They killed him,' she said calmly. 'My baby. They made him dead and I wasn't there and I can still *smell* him on me.'

She started rocking again.

224

'Oh Grud,' Armitage said softly. He looked at the wrecked woman and tried to think of anything at all to say.

And then the alarms went off.

The Undercity, MC1

Through the undercity tunnels, an integral light-source in her cybernetic body casting a pale bluish glow before her. The gun drawn and ready, one hand cradled in the other.

The tunnels had been here for centuries, millennia even; extending and evolving and reforming. There are things down here, stranger and more abstract than alligators and pigs and drowned foetal matter, far stranger than the Undercity gangs; a juxtaposition of brickwork, the trapped curve of an invisible signal: the automemes of a buried city.

She heard the roar and the rattle of something mechanical running distant through the rock, saw the glitter of rat eyes looking up at her as she intersected old sewers. Rusting iron catwalks and stone bridges, some relatively recent, others hundreds if not thousands of years old.

Chaotic electrical activity in her cybernetic head; she felt the physical pressure of connections firing. Reptile backbrain and mammal and simian. Ghosts under glass. Picosecond flashes of image and sensation and impulse: fear and hunger and glassy pain.

She was close now. Ahead, a pale phosphorescent glow. She switched off her lights and headed towards it, following the gentle curve of the tunnel.

A ragged figure slumped against the wall of the tunnel, its broken mouth hanging open, its nose and the left side of its face mashed and bruised. Quite dead. Her body lay limp beside it.

A construct. A paraspace construct.

It was as if it was made of glass: perfectly clear, its neurostructure and pulmonary system suspended in it, twisting sparking wormholes filled with luminous fluid.

A pulsing analogue of a heart filled her chest cavity, bulging, bulging, pressing against the walls. Things moved inside it, tearing at the surface. The tunnel reverberated with its beat.

Karyn raised her gun.

Something pushed itself from the swollen, glowing heart, a tiny shapeless mass of insect legs and teeth. It bored through the gelid body, expanding. Another followed it. Then another. And another.

Karyn pulled the trigger.

Slugs stitched into the body – and passed right through like there was nothing there, smashing into the wall of the tunnel in a spray of fractured brick and cement.

The heart split open and hundreds of thousands of tiny Medusa-forms spilled out, spreading through the body, expanding explosively, filling the body up.

The Big House

The hole was perfectly delineated, sharp-edged, the mouth of a tunnel stretching to infinity, a wormhole bored into the solid golden light. Moloch drifted towards it, slipping through the half-felt bodies of dead imaginary creatures.

'The Core's in there,' Lucy Too's voice said.

226

'Sucked in there alive and screaming. I can feel it. We have to go there.'

Moloch floated into the tunnel, ambient light from the bright solid womanshape behind him: he could see himself and Lucy Too again. She was pale now, thinner than she had been before, older. Suggestions of lines around the eyes and mouth. She seemed to be in her mid-twenties.

'Are you all right?' I asked her. 'What happened to you?'

'Something burned in me,' she said simply. 'It hurt.'

'Why didn't you *say* something?'

She shrugged. An adult gesture. 'It's not important. We have to find the Core before it dies. We have to bring it out.'

The walls of the tunnel were crystalline, diamond-hard. Lights flared behind them, rippled, flashed past Moloch as he jacked up his speed. Heading for the centre. Heading for the Core.

Lucy Too looked up at him, hair streaming in a nonexistent slipstream. 'We're close now,' she said. 'We're very close.'

A change in the quality of the light ahead. He sensed a dead end of some kind ahead of him. The walls of the tunnel opened out into a chamber.

Extruded spiderstrands running from the walls, twisting themselves into a solidified knot in the centre. Hung from the web, dry husks: a collapsed and leathery sac, mouths hanging from it on stalks; a reptilian skin hanging from a crude wooden cross; a thin man in the ashy remains of a black suit, ruptured mouth hanging open in a huge flap.

The lump of clotted gossamer in the centre of the

chamber bulged and relaxed, bulged and relaxed, light pulsing within.

'The Core,' Lucy Too said.

There was something rough and hungry in her voice. Moloch looked down at her and saw she was grinning, licking her lips. Her teeth seemed very sharp.

'I told you I was going to eat it,' she said. 'I'm going to eat it now, kill the Core and eat it. Eat it all *up*.'

She had an old woman's face now, staring at him through a paper-thin mask of youth: spiteful and full of an obscene and senile viciousness.

'You can't,' he said desperately. 'It's alive. You can't – ' He lurched back into the tunnel – and then her hands were around his throat, digging in with an inhuman strength.

'It's dead and rotting,' Lucy Too hissed. 'A light burning in an empty shell. It's my light. *Mine*.'

The pressure increased. Moloch tried to change into a new form, tried to pull the feeling of something else out of himself, but he looked into her dead blank eyes and there was nothing there.

'I needed you,' Lucy Too said. Her voice was cracked and dry and she was thinner now, almost skeletal. 'I needed you to bring me here, but I don't need you anymore. Let me go. Let me go now and I'll let you live.'

Moloch let go of her. She hung in the air for a moment, weightless, snarling at him, then launched herself into the chamber, caught hold of a gossamer strand and hauled herself towards the Core.

Moloch stayed where he was, just watching her, and all he could feel was relief. The Core was going to die now, killed by something that might have been itself once: the decision and the guilt were taken out of his hands.

Lucy Too had reached the Core. She plunged her hands into its cocoon, tearing shreds of congealed web away in a grey cloud of flakes. Moloch heard a faint crackling, like lobstershells breaking. She stuck her head into the crack, pulling it apart.

Light burst from the shell, bright and hard and sharp. It wheeled, sliced through the screaming Lucy Too, slicing her layer by layer, peeling her.

And when she was nothing but folds of flesh it entered her, a small blue sun infusing her, cohering her, drawing her together.

She stopped screaming, hung motionless before the cocoon. It rippled weakly, the light inside it fading to black. The pulsing of its inner walls accelerated wildly, fibrillating.

And then it split down the middle.

It folded back on itself, turned itself inside out, ripping itself into shreds.

Swirling multicoloured light behind it. The parareality.

Moloch launched myself towards Lucy Too, spiderstrands snapping and whiplashing around him. He pulled her back from the expanding hole. She was hot to the touch, something burning inside her and through her.

Her face was as he had first seen it: a girl of maybe sixteen. Her eyes were closed and she smiled faintly, sleeping rather than unconscious. There was something else there, too – a softening of the predatory features, the impression of some emotional depth that hadn't been there before, as though her melding with the Core had transmuted her somehow. She stirred and murmured something, but didn't wake up.

A wrenching behind him, a tearing – and suddenly something was sucking at him, sucking him back towards the hole.

A strand of the web whiplashed in front of him. He grabbed for it, wrapped it around his hand. Lucy Too slithered from him; he grabbed hold of her leather jacket, hauled her back and slung her over his shoulder.

And then he looked back:

A solid wall of Medusa, millions of them, unending animated abstract forms: a shredded male hand machine and insect clusters wound with neon . . . a clenching hand the fractured clenching he . . . something *inside* he . . .

They surged forward.

Terminal Shock

Across the city, across the world, thousands upon thousands of children, their brains sliced and sutured into new shapes: crazy-paving quasi-axons radiating from a cybernetically enhanced brainstem: mutated, enlarged pituitary and hypothalamus and corpus callosum.

Patchwork approximations of the changes spliced into their genes, the structure that would form an integral part of the next generation, the generation they had grown up to sire.

Some of them coped with the voices and the impulses and the terrifying hallucinations in their heads. Some of them didn't.

New York 1936

They found construction elevators operated by counterbalanced sandbags. They ascended through the partially completed construction, stone-cladding and glass giving way to rough timber platforms and untreated iron.

The killer was waiting. He stood, relaxed, between two load bearing supports. He was naked. His scorched flesh hung from him, occasionally spitting and hissing as though frying in fat.

Dredd pulled his Lawgiver and stepped forward onto a catwalk. The night was perfectly still. Heavy frost caked and sparkled on the freezing iron. Above, the stars shone with an absolute and diamond-hard clarity. From below, the faint chug of automobile traffic.

The killer frowned. 'Are you a demon?' he croaked. 'Are you truly a demon? Have you come to bear me to Hell for my sins, which are numerous?

'You have not.'

The discharge arced to the Lawgiver, fusing its circuits and sending it flying. Treasure, working round what she hoped to Grud was the blind side, saw it clatter against the supports for a stairwell before being lost forever.

'You have not,' the killer said, quite calmly – and leapt, taking Dredd in the chest and bearing him off the catwalk to land hard on a horizontal girder.

'You have *not*.' And with lightning speed, faster than any human being could react to, the killer shattered Dredd's already damaged leg with three sledgehammer blows.

The Undercity, MC1

Big tunnel big tunnel big black tunnel opening up behind her, something tearing from her, sucked into the tunnel, falling away.

Her cybernetic body was shivering and jerking as though electrocuted, machine pistol still clutched in one flailing hand, firing blindly. The spurting bullets sliced the top of the head of the dead man sprawled against the wall of the tunnel – and as the blackness washed over her, Karyn saw that the dead man was *moving*.

The Bunker

The roar of turbines, the shrieking of an alarm, mechanical rather than transputronic. The tiles under him were shaking, intangible hammerblows jarring the base of his skull.

'Jovus!' Armitage shouted to where Sela stood with her hands pressed to her ears.

It was obvious that she hadn't heard him. He waved frantically to attract her attention, panto-mimed that it might be an idea to think about leaving. She nodded. Her eyes were wide.

The lights were pale and flickering. The archaic monitors of the bunker blazed; random characters and numbers scrolling too fast for the eye to catch. On a paraspace monitor, though neither Judge knew what it meant, concentric bright white circles con-tracted across a field of yellow to a dazzling pinpoint. The monitor burned out with a crack, overloaded.

The throb of turbines accelerated and relays tripped out, plunging the bunker into darkness. The whisper of air conditioning vents ceased, noticeable only now that it had stopped.

Purple lights spun before Armitage's retinae; he lurched against a bench, a sharp corner scraping his ribcage. Something heavy toppled to the floor with a crash. His groping fingers found Sela.

He moved forward cautiously, gripping Sela by the hand, free arm outstretched, glass crunching under his feet, eventually coming to a smooth metallic wall. He followed it round to a door.

For one awful moment he thought the lock would operate electrically, that they were trapped here in an airtight box and would suffocate in the dark. But the door slid back easily. The sound of the turbines was almost deafening now.

A corridor, sparking arclight flaring from a door farther down and casting flickering blue ripples across the walls. They made their way to the door, moving faster now that they could see.

A small chamber. Something bloated and semi-organic in a tank of cloudy fluid. The fluid in the tank seethed, the white flesh shuddering.

It collapsed, imploded. The crunch of impacted bone. A perfect haemorrhaging sphere.

Pale light burst from it, discrete beams, thousands of them, radiating on a horizontal plane.

The beams sliced through Armitage and Sela, and Armitage felt white fire in his veins. He felt a sucking: something shooting through the strands: a thousand frantic snatches of identity and information bursting through him.

Somebody was saying that it wasn't his fault, it wasn't his . . . Fading.

The feel of a dislocated ankle, a shattered fibula;

233

something sliding in a hot wet bloody hole; the dead weight of the shame that made him pull himself into himself and never come out; the hunger.

And then it was gone. The bright globe bubbled, shrieked; a thousand scraped and tortured voices drowning out the descending whine of the turbines. The light faded leaving a dark and fibrous surface, ridged and pitted like a scab.

Silence. Then something churned inside the globe and it began to burn: a big sun machine, blinding white.

It burst from the tank, an explosion of steel and glass and fluid. Armitage shoved Sela out of the way and threw himself flat as it streaked past him, his trenchcoat igniting in superheated air.

The globe hit the wall, ate through it; the smell of baking ceramic and brick.

And then it was gone.

Armitage struggled out of his jacket. He threw it away from him. Sela was starting to smoulder, and rolled determinedly to crush it out.

And then the lights came on.

New York 1936

Dredd gazed up into the smiling face of the killer. The killer smiled down, showed him his own boot knife. The killer smiled kindly.

Off to one side, through the blood roaring in his ears, he heard the voice of Treasure Steel. 'Try this one on for size, matey.'

There was a *ftuum*. Something metallic streaked for the killer and struck him squarely in the chest with a crunch. Hooks extended on microservos, sunk themselves into his flesh, securing the projectile immovably.

The projectile squealed, and then it began to speak: *'I'm a thirty second bomb! I'm a thirty second bomb! Twenty-nine. Twenty-eight. Twenty-seven. Twenty-six . . .'*

'Smart anti-personnel device,' Treasure called. 'You get to program it with your own routine. Pretty neat, eh?'

The killer squawked, tried to pluck ineffectually at the smart bomb in his chest, but to no avail.

'Sixteen. Fifteen. Fourteen. Thirteen . . .'

And now, the killer's patina of gentleness finally and irrevocably gave way. There was no sense of transition: his face simply split into a twisted snarl of fury. A rasping howl ripped from his throat and he brought down the knife.

There was no time for thought. Dredd simply rolled off the girder. He plunged three metres – and his flailing hands brushed a hanging rope. He grabbed for it desperately, gauntleted fingers closing upon it.

The rope was run through a block and tackle. For another second he continued to fall – and there was a *clunk* from above.

The sudden slow to a stop nearly pulled his arm out of its socket. He slammed into the side of a vertical girder with a clang. Still gripping the rope, he wound the slack around his free hand.

Then he looked up. The rope had been attached to an iron bucket, which had wedged in the block and tackle with a small spray of the rivets it contained, the force of impact almost shearing off the makeshift bracket from which it depended. Dredd wrapped an arm and his good leg around the vertical girder and clung on.

All of this had taken maybe five seconds. The killer still clung to his perch, having lost both his balance, momentarily, when Dredd had disappeared from under him, and also the knife, which went over the side as he was grabbing for support.

And the smart bomb was still counting: '*Eight. Seven. Six. Five. Four. Three. SYSTEM MAL-FUNCTION! SYSTEM MALFUNCTION! Three. Three. Three. Three. Three . . .*'

A grin of evil delight passed across the killer's face.

'Do you see?' he screamed down at Dredd. 'I am safe in the arms of my God! You cannot kill *me*. I am inviolable!'

'*Only joking*,' said the smart bomb, and detonated.

Almost Everywhere

When, all those years before, the unknown origina-tors of Special Services Section 8 had seen the Medusa for what it was, they had realised that this was a threat against which every resource must be brought, every possible weapon used, every moral or technical crime permissable. It was a question of life or death, not simply of one species or one world – but of life or death for an entire universe.

And so a plan of extreme complexity and astonish-ing cruelty was formulated. Children were modified to present a tempting target for the Medusa, an unlocked door with a metaphorical neon arrow point-ing to it. A trap with the children as bait.

A trap with a sting in the tail.

* * *

Armitage gazed around at the chamber and the lifeless consoles, playing his torch over the archaic surfaces. 'Just some old sound-studio, by the look of the thing. It's not important. What did you say?'

'I . . .' Sela smiled slightly and shook her head. 'I was just saying that it's good to be doing the real stuff for a change. I mean, when I think of all those years having to live with that little drokker Raan. Just thank Grud he didn't get me pregnant, is all. I think that could have really messed me up. Up the *spart*, eh? Isn't that what you Brits call it?'

'Only if we want to sound like Dick Van Dyke in *Mary Poppins*,' said Armitage.

And so the children grew up and had children of their own. Genetic drift saw to it that their modifications spread through the gene-pool, thinly in places, more concentrated in others. Those who by random selection most closely approximated the original prototypes would eventually be incorporated into the new world order as Psi Judges.

This was not the primary function however. The primary function lay in the Bunker, and its substations scattered throughout the world.

When the walls of reality began to fragment, the bunker had allowed itself to be activated, fed out its electromagnetic feelers and hooked itself into the minds it needed: the psis first, the sensitives second, running through the hierarchies of genetic concentration to the dregs.

It had twisted their minds and fed off their madness, converting what it fed upon to an energy that had no knowable name.

* * *

Somehow the tunnels were easier to get round now. After a while they found Karyn and Thead. Thead was dead, half his head blown away. It seemed that in his last seconds he had been trying to crawl towards Karyn.

'Serves the bastard right,' said Armitage.

There was no sign of whatever had killed him. Armitage glanced idly down at an old collection of scraps. It seemed that someone had been trying to wrap discarded metal tubing with sacking and then had simply wandered off and forgotten about it.

Karyn was pale and breathing deeply. She stirred. She opened her eyes.

'Hello,' she said calmly. 'You're . . . Armitage, is that right? And you're Sela Kane. What the drokk's been happening?'

'I gather that you went out of your head for a while,' said Armitage, 'and the god-botherer there happened to find you.'

He looked down again at the remains of Thead. 'Ah, well, it saves Brit-Cit the cost of a one-way ticket, anyway.'

They made their way upward to the exit hatch. It was only after they were safely through and into the precarious safety of the Mega-City itself that they stopped to wonder how they could have walked through such a perilous place as the Undercity so flippantly.

Certain Undercity inhabitants, who had covertly escorted them all the way up on an impulse they could not have explained, returned to the depths to resume their unending wars.

* * *

238

*The Bunker had hit upon a small problem at the start.
The psis of Mega-City One had been cushioned by
the drugs they took – and while this was perfectly all
right if one merely wishes to feed off them, there were
certain procedures that required a greater level of
sophistication. It had only been by pure luck that the
Bunker had managed to locate and instill certain
information in the minds of a pair with the right set
of parameters. (The Bunker had indulged in a little
suppression of its own. Karyn had never wondered
exactly why the simulacrum of Moloch in the Think
Tank had suddenly mentioned that breaking out must
be done without the drugs from left field.)*

*It had led its people through the maze of itself both
overtly, instilling knowledge directly in their minds,
and covertly: leaving the way clear for the Medusa to
attack Karyn, guiding Moloch through the Big House
of Karyn's brain by way of the construct Lucy Too.
It had allowed the meta-being of the Medusa to take
possession of Absolom Leviticus Thead because it
was necessary that Karyn's body be brought down
here to be confronted by her actual self. It had merely
implanted an automatic urge to look for the safe
dark.*

*And, at last, when the Medusa had made its
ultimate advance, all had been in its place.*

And across the world, people woke up from their
madness as though from a bad dream. Those who
had been screaming with horror until their lungs
bled, shook themselves and shrugged and wondered
what had given them such a turn. Over the next few
days, from Lhasa to the Pan Andes Conurb, the
Resyk Plants worked overtime processing unex-

pected millions who just happened to have sort of died.

Only nobody thought much about it.

The Bunker channelled its stolen power, the power it had stolen from the madness of the world – channelled it in one white-hot burst through Karyn's nearby ego-construct and into her vacated physical body.

The thousands upon thousands of automemes locked in Karyn's physical brain were fuelled with energy – blazed with it. They burst from their individual niches in the Big House and streamed for the Cellar, focused themselves through Moloch's construct and blasted into the paraspace, destroying every Medusa cell in their path.

It was impossible, of course, to mortally wound the meta-being, the true Medusa – but it lurched back, streamed away through the paraspace to a place of relative safety.

It had learnt the power of the sting. It knew that these little creatures could hurt.

In his room in the Mega-City Psi-division, Moloch rubbed at gritty eyes. The fever had left him now.

He tried to remember the visions he had seen in the throes of his fever: something about a house, something about a room that talked. Somehow, the way that dream logic does, it had all seemed so natural at the time. And he couldn't rid himself of the feeling that there was something vital he had seen, something that needed to be told.

Ah, well, probably not important.

240

Want to bet? said the voice of Lucy Too in his head.

The Medusa would try again, of course. That was a large part of what it was, integral to it. But in human terms, on human time-scales, it would be centuries before it would try again.

Its work done, the Bunker tried as best it could to repair the damage it had done, so far as it could be repaired, wiping memories where possible, restoring the living to themselves.

And, when it noticed, it attempted to do some small good.

And then it switched itself off.

New York 1936

Treasure sat on the girder and swung her feet, looking out in the city. The sun was coming up.

Beside her, Dredd sat leant back against a vertical, examining his wrecked leg. 'I think they're going to have to crash-graft,' he said grimly.

After the killer had gone to pieces, as it were, Treasure had clambered down to help Dredd haul himself to a more secure position. This left them with the problem of negotiating the half-completed structure of the building to reach the construction elevators. Treasure thought she could do it on her own, but with Dredd crippled there was no way.

'Y'know,' she said thoughtfully, 'what with this Albert Fish guy splattered over a couple of blocks, doesn't that sort of change history? Wasn't he executed?'

'That's the least of our problems,' said Dredd. 'If we get back, what we do is gestate a body from the genetic samples we took, scorch it up a little and then we send it back a split-second after he originally left.' He scowled down at the city below: the crawling traffic and ant-like people streaming along the sidewalks, the knot of people and vehicles clustered around the base of the building.

'They can see we're up here,' he said. 'They can see what came down. At the moment it's just some other guy who took a high dive – but Grud only knows what's going to happen if they pull us in.'

There was a small explosion of air – and suddenly, hovering rather ineptly on a pair of impellers lashed to the frame, was a Time Pod – one of the basic prototype vehicles that were as far as Mega-City One research had pushed the fledgling art of temporal engineering. The Pod wobbled slightly, then a hatch swung open and a slightly green-looking Armitage stuck his head out.

'Oh Jovus,' he said. 'Excuse me one moment.'

He leant over the side and heaved the contents of his stomach in the general direction of the people below.

'Blimey!' he said rubbing at his mouth. 'They said the displacement was a killer, and how right they were. Mornin', Chuckles. Your cab awaits.'

'How did you find us?' Treasure exclaimed.

'Ah,' said Armitage. 'Now, I'll bet you'll be wanting to hear such a tale of deduction and ingenuity that'll make your hair stand on end. I expect you'll wish to hear of how by pure inductive reasoning and not a little luck we managed to pinpoint the exact source of – '

'What you're saying is,' Dredd cut in shortly, 'that you went ahead to when we got back and asked us.'

Armitage deflated slightly. 'I cannot tell a lie. The old ones are the best. Do you want to go home now, or what?'

Sector One, MC1

The stratoliners were running again. Dredd escorted Armitage and Steel to the stratoport for the simple reason, he averred, that he didn't trust the pair of them one micromillimetre and he didn't want to let them out of his sight. His leg had been amputated at the thigh and he had been fitted with a temporary prosthetic which would support him and keep the tissue of the stump alive while a limb-graft was prepared from his own genetic material.

As they had travelled through the city, and now in the departure lounge of the stratoport, they noticed a kind of unnatural calm, as though after a thunderstorm: vast energies had been expended and now everything was cool and subdued.

'Y'know,' said Treasure thoughtfully, 'I can't help thinking that all this is my fault. I mean, if I hadn't zapped this Albert Fish guy, then he would have stayed on this timeline and all these disruptions wouldn't have happened.'

Armitage shrugged. 'Don't worry about it. You were just one link in a whole chain of coincidences. Fault doesn't come into it.'

For a moment, Armitage remembered something – something about a feeling of being guided, *manipulated*, glowing consoles in a golden chamber. And then it was gone.

He jerked a thumb in the direction of Dredd, who was busting a vaguely senile old woman for littering with her hottie wrapper.

'He's got the right idea, I think,' he said. 'The only thing you can do, whatever happens, is be yourself as hard as possible – as much as anyone ever can be.' He paused thoughtfully and then smiled slightly. 'And the moment we get out of Mega-City One jurisdiction I think I'm going to be myself with a big bottle of scotch.'